Christmas of Love

The Sunshine Breakfast Club (Book4)

KARICE BOLTON

Christmas of Love

Cover Design by Didi Wahyudi

Exterior: Adobe Stock © PixelShot

Interior Formatting: BB Formatting Adobe Stock © Mimi Art Smile

Copyright © 2023 Karice Bolton

ISBN: 979-8-9872814-5-1

Christmas of Love

For My Family,

You're my everything!

Christmas of Love

Chapter One

Daisy

'Tis the season to be jolly, Fa-la-la-la-la, la-la-la…

Silence.

The radio stopped.

"No, no, no. No. You need to start, Foxy. You need to start." I gently banged my fist on the steering wheel as lovingly as possible and groaned.

The ignition wouldn't even turn over in my trusty Subaru wagon.

I could see my breath in the air inside my car.

1

My wipers were frozen on the windshield.

If this were a hint of the holiday season to come, I'd gladly fly to the Bahamas.

I glanced in my rearview mirror to see the lights still on at the community center and the Sunshine Breakfast Club gleefully gathering in the window.

They were always so perky, those people.

"Ugh, this isn't what I need right now." I had thirty minutes to get to my bartending shift at the resort.

I'd promised Millie that I'd stop by the book club to deliver my famous candy cane fudge, but I just didn't have time this month to join in on their monthly reading selection.

And now, I had to walk back in with my tail between my legs and ask for help.

But at what cost?

There was always a catch with the Sunshine Breakfast Club. I knew this all too well because I was often one of the conspirators orchestrating something behind the scenes to bring two unsuspecting souls together.

I chuckled and unbuckled, hopping out of my car as the first flake landed on my nose. I should have just agreed to read the book.

This was Christmas karma.

I tied my wool scarf tighter, zipped up my puffy, red,

goose-down jacket, and trudged across the parking lot.

Yanking the door open, I smelled the sweet cinnamon apple cider drifting through the air. Laughter jangled down the hall as I shut the door behind me with a thud.

They were obviously having a better night than I was.

The giant Christmas tree in the corner of the lobby twinkled its red and green lights with sparkling holiday tags dangling for those families in need. I'd already picked one family from the tree and couldn't wait to select another. I always tried to buy toys for kiddos whose families might need a little extra. I remembered all too well what it was like growing up in hard times, and Christmas only highlighted the fact.

I pulled off my gloves and walked down the hall to the meeting room where the Sunshine Breakfast Club had gathered.

About twenty members had made it to the meeting. Two tables with green plaid tablecloths had been pushed together in the back of the room and were filled with food. A miniature tree with tiny book ornaments had been propped on the drinks table, along with a tray of cookies.

My stomach growled just as Millie's gaze landed on me. She was the ringleader—I mean, book club president. She'd earned her title years ago, and nobody would ever dare

3

take it away. Her silver hair had been cut into a bob. She'd managed to put two poofy red barrettes on each side, but the topper was her flashing Rudolph sweater. The blinking nose put me in a trance as she grabbed my cold hand and cupped it to make it warmer.

"Welcome back, Daisy. Did you change your mind about this month's book?" She grinned with the wisdom of being in her eighth decade on this planet.

My cheeks flushed. "No. Foxy won't start."

Millie's white brows rose. "Foxy?"

I shook my head. "Oh, sorry. My car won't start. I had it idling, and then it just died, and now it won't turn over."

I glanced around the room to see the Bailey sisters. Nina, Grace, and Maya gave a quick wave before turning back to their plates of food. Maybe one of them could give me a ride.

"That's a shame, dear." She squeezed my hand. "But do you know what that tells me?"

I chuckled, taking off my knit hat. "I can only imagine."

"You're meant to be here." Millie snapped her fingers, and Abby from the coffee shop came over with a cup of tea.

I took the cup and grinned at Abby. "Thank you." But

then I turned my attention to Millie. "But I'm actually meant to be at Buttercup Lake Resort in less than twenty minutes."

"Oh, you're in a real pickle."

I laughed, nodding. "It appears so."

"Well, the resort's only ten minutes away. We're about to chat about the overall themes of the next book selection we're about to read."

"But…" I started again.

Millie shook her head and looped her fingers through mine. "But nothing. Come on over, Daisy."

"What's the book even about?" I asked as she led me to an empty chair.

"Well, we haven't started it yet." She reached for a paperback turned upside down on the chair beside me. "But it's the perfect holiday romance called *The Little Christmas Bar Around the Corner.*"

I chuckled. "That's one I haven't heard of. I thought you guys might be reading *A Christmas Carol* or something."

"We need something light and festive," Millie said, glancing at Maya, who took a seat next to her. "Okay, Ladies. Let's gather around."

I looked around the room and shook my head. "Do you think we could see who could drive me to the resort first? I hate to ask, but it's really important that I get there on time.

I'll make more fudge for whoever drives me."

To say I was embarrassed was an understatement, but I absolutely needed to get to my job on time. I was the only bartender on duty since it was a Tuesday night, right before a blizzard was supposed to slam into our area.

Millie frowned and shook her head. "Oh, no, dear. All the ladies here must join in the planning for our holiday party and come up with the reading schedule, but..." She turned in her seat and smiled at Maya. "Didn't you say that Hunter was swinging by?"

Hunter Knox.

Oh, no.

Not Hunter Knox, ex-boss, gorgeous mess of a man.

What was he even doing in Buttercup Lake? His bar was down in Madison.

I let out a sigh and chuckled. "I'd rather just miss my shift."

Millie rolled her eyes and looked at Maya. "Don't be so dramatic. He's on his way, right?"

She nodded, taking a bite of Kringle. "Yeah. Cash had already asked him to swing by and grab a sample of gingerbread beer from him. It's in my trunk."

"Gingerbread beer?" I cocked my head slightly.

"Don't ask. Cash is trying his hand at home brewing

6

and…"

I chuckled. "Gotcha."

Cash Knox and Maya were the perfect match, and truth be told, the Sunshine Breakfast Club had plenty to do with that coupling. This book club was skilled at what they did to the poor, unsuspecting love birds.

Time and again.

"Anyway, he should be here any second," Maya explained.

All the women were finding their seats with plates full of food, and my stomach sank.

First of all, Hunter probably didn't even know I existed. I'd worked for him less than a month last Christmas, and he'd barely uttered a word to me. Instead of looking *at* me, he looked *through* me.

Second of all, I remembered Hunter all too well. If I were ever to have had a crush on an older guy, it would be him.

But I didn't.

Sparkling blue eyes to match the rest of the Knox brothers. A carefree attitude that was infectious. A laugh that made my stomach flutter.

And his muscular build that left little to the imagination.

7

Ugh.

Hunter Knox.

I shuddered at the thought of him coming to my rescue.

And what if his on-and-off girlfriend was with him?

Another shudder ran through me.

Breanna. Or was it Briella? Maybe Cruella?

I couldn't remember, but I did recall how mean and grumpy she was to anyone who happened to be within a ten-foot radius of her or Hunter.

Fun times.

"You know what? I'm totally fine. I'll just go try to start Foxy again," I assured Maya and Millie. I didn't need a ride from Hunter. I didn't need anything from Hunter. I didn't need a holiday card. I didn't need a job.

Maya looked surprised. "I thought you enjoyed working down in Madison. Did my brother-in-law scare you away?"

"I'm pretty sure I annoyed him. He barely looked at me when I was there. And he was the one who signed my paychecks." I laughed. "So, I'm not sure he'd actually want to give me a ride."

Millie chuckled and glanced over my shoulder. "Then it's like a fresh start. You're not his employee. He's not your boss."

I scowled. "What do you mean, a fresh start? There is no start. There was only an end. An end to my time bartending in the city. Besides, Hunter is just one of many obnoxiously good-looking men who mindlessly wander around Wisconsin." I shrugged. "Not to mention, I'm sure he has a fantastic ego. But please don't tell him or his brother that. I don't want to hurt their feelings."

"We won't." Maya's lips were pressed into a thin line, and her eyes were as large as saucers as she stared behind me.

My shoulders slumped. "Hunter is standing behind me, isn't he?"

Millie chuckled as Maya stood, rubbing her hands together before reaching for her coat on the chair. "Hey there, Hunter. Your brother has some beer for you to try."

"Oh, yeah?" Sexiness dripped from his deep voice while I glared at Millie.

She knew he'd been there.

Millie chuckled and squeezed my hands. "Don't you just love this time of year? Joy just bounces off the walls."

"I don't know about joy, but something is certainly bouncing around."

Millie eyed the man behind me. "Hey, Hunter. Would you do me a favor?"

"Sure thing, Millie." The roughness in his voice made my belly dip into a tingly mess.

I refused to look behind me.

This wasn't good.

He still had the same effect on me.

It was the weirdest thing. Being a bartender, I was used to being hit on. I'd become immune to good-looking men trying to pick me up. But with Hunter Knox, all I could think about was what it would be like to be kissed by him.

There was no in-between with him. No wooing, no courting, dating, chilling, just a kiss. That was all I thought about.

A kiss.

Which meant he had to be trouble because in my book, personality was what trumped everything else. But with Hunter, I didn't have the foggiest clue about his personality other than that he had an ego the size of Texas with an aloofness that barked at me.

Not good.

"Would you mind taking Daisy to her shift over at the resort? This time, try not to leave such a bad taste in her mouth." Millie grinned like the Cheshire Cat. "You know, try to let some of our Christmas cheer rub off on you. She promised she'd make her famous fudge for whoever drove her."

He laughed. "For the record, I do remember you, Daisy. And Merry Christmas."

I clenched my eyes shut and willed myself to wipe away the embarrassment.

"Merry Christmas, Hunter," I said through gritted teeth.

Did he actually remember me, or was he trying to save face in front of Millie and everyone else?

Millie chuckled as my eyes blinked open, and I stood from the chair and slowly turned around.

Hunter Knox looked even better than I had remembered.

Double dang it.

His blue eyes darn near twinkled as he watched me zip my coat, tug on my hat, and flop my scarf over my shoulder.

"I really don't want to be an imposition," I said, shaking my head. "I can figure something else out."

"You'd never be an imposition, Daisy. You never have been, and you never will be." His eyes stayed on mine, and a flare of electricity shot through me. "I'm sorry if I ever made you feel that way. The bar can be crazy at times. That was never my intention."

Millie patted my shoulder. "Good. Good. See? There's the start. You two be careful on the ride over there."

I glanced at Maya, who waved us over to the door as she laughed. She turned around in the lobby and grinned, whispering, "I don't think that could have gotten any more awkward."

I chuckled, glancing at Hunter behind us. "Let's not jinx it. I'm sure I can come up with a way."

We walked through the lobby, and Hunter hurried in front of us to open the door. The chill of the evening air pricked my exposed skin as Maya pointed at her car.

But Hunter stood outside with nothing more than low-slung jeans, a grey flannel, and a light jacket. It was as if he were impervious to the cold, just a big boulder of a man unaware of the elements.

"The blizzard is on its way." I shivered as I glanced at Foxy betraying me in the parking lot.

"It sure is," Maya agreed. "Come on, Hunter. Let me give you the beer so you can message your brother tonight about how fabulous it is. And I can get back inside without turning blue."

Hunter laughed, and I noticed his easy smile. He seemed a lot more relaxed than when I'd last seen him.

Not that it mattered.

He nodded. "Will do."

Maya opened her trunk and gave Hunter a box that clanked as he adjusted it.

I stared at my car, silently willing it to come alive for me.

"Thanks, Maya. Tell my brother I'll text him with my unbiased opinion." He turned to me and smiled. "And we'd better get you to work."

"How'd you know I wasn't headed to the resort for a holiday party?"

Hunter grinned and shrugged. "Just a hunch. You were a bartender there before you came to Madison, so I assume you're still one after you left."

"I'll let you two be. Drive safely." She gave her brother-in-law a pat on the shoulder and smiled at me. "Thanks for taking Daisy to her shift. I'd better get back inside before Millie gets after me."

"See ya later, Maya." I waved and turned to Hunter. "If you don't mind, I'm just going to give Foxy another try so you don't have to drive me."

His brows raised. "Pardon?"

My cheeks flushed. "Oh, sorry. Foxy is my Subaru. She died and wouldn't start. That's why I need a ride."

He chuckled, and his eyes stayed on mine. "Maybe if

you gave her a name with more dignity, she wouldn't have died on you."

My gaze sharpened on Hunter. "I'll have you know that she was an absolute fox in her time."

Hunter's mouth curved into a perfect smile, and his gorgeous eyes narrowed on me. "Which decade was that?"

I slid into the seat and turned the ignition to hear absolutely nothing in return, and now I only had ten minutes to get to work.

He'd put the box in his vehicle, which happened to be next to mine, and stood next to my open car door.

Hunter winked and held out his hand for me. "Foxy doesn't sound very lively. Let me get you to your job. Come on. We'll get this sorted tomorrow."

We?

There was no we about Hunter and me.

But whatever. I just needed to get to Buttercup Lake Resort.

I nodded, sliding my key out of the ignition before I gripped his hand and stood.

"Suddenly chivalrous?" I joked as his eyes caught mine.

"Must be the season," he teased, dropping his hand from mine. "But I certainly didn't make a great impression on you. I'm sorry about that."

"Nah. You were fine. Just busy at the bar like you mentioned. Anyway, thanks for taking me. I owe you a coffee or something."

"Don't give it a second thought, but I think fudge was mentioned." He opened the passenger door for me in his white G Wagon. "The seats should warm you right up."

I chuckled, sliding into his SUV. "Oh, fancy."

Hunter shook his head and climbed into the driver's side. "This car wasn't my idea, but Brielle insisted this was *the one* when my other car died."

Ah, Brielle. That was her name.

I should have known it wasn't Cruella.

"Well, the seats are very lovely." Which was a total lie because the moment he started the SUV, the slow creep of warmth puddling underneath me made me think I'd drunk too much coffee and didn't make it to the ladies' room in time.

"I've never been into them, to be honest. I don't like how it feels." He glanced over at me as he pulled out of the parking lot. "It makes me think I'm pissing."

I snorted and rolled my eyes. "You've always been one to be direct."

He slowly pulled onto the main road. "Yeah? How should I have said it?"

I chuckled. "I don't know. Maybe fib like I did and say you loved them."

He chuckled, and I felt a sudden change between us.

"You know, Daisy, I hope I can make things up to you. I never meant to make you feel that way. I didn't know I was that lousy of a boss."

"You weren't that bad." I laughed, shaking my head. "I'm just shocked you remembered my name."

Chapter Two

Hunter

What was it she said?

Egotistical?

Can't remember his own employees' names? Her name?

I shook my head and sighed. But she did say I was obnoxiously good-looking, so that might be in my favor.

Popping the cap from my brother's beer, I took a swig and almost spat out the bitter liquid. My lips puckered as the sour beer coated my tongue, and I leaned over my kitchen sink.

Just in case.

"Yikes." After a few minutes, I wiped my mouth with the back of my hand and set the bottle on the counter, unsure of what to tell my brother.

But it was awful.

The Grinch suddenly flashed on the television in my family room as Daisy's words mingled with my thoughts.

She'd said I was too direct. Was that true? Wasn't that better than beating around the bush?

I stared at the beer bottle my brother brewed and sighed as I grabbed a glass of water to rinse out my mouth.

Wouldn't it be better to tell him not to serve that to anyone else?

Or...

Maybe I should let someone else be the bad guy.

But then my brother wouldn't be able to trust my opinion.

I flipped on the light in the family room, walked over to my couch, and sat down to stare at the television.

Why was I letting this woman's words complicate my life?

But I knew the answer.

The moment I heard Daisy's voice at the community center, I was immediately pulled back to those amazing four weeks when she worked at my bar.

She was so chipper, happy, and full of life.

Daisy damn near glowed when she rushed from one side of the counter to the other.

But I'd done too good of a job pretending that being around her didn't affect every part of my world.

Whenever I'd heard her laughing with a patron or flipping a flirty response to one of her coworkers, I wanted to join in so badly, but I knew my place.

And my ex was usually lurking somewhere in the bar.

So, I stayed away, didn't speak to Daisy unless it was an absolute must, and breathed a sigh of relief when her tenure was through.

I thought back to the first time Millie mentioned hiring Daisy in Madison for the holidays. I thought for sure that they were trying to hook us up. My family was less than enthralled with Brielle, so I assumed the Sunshine Breakfast Club had made us their next match.

They had a nasty habit of pairing people up around town.

That club was always up to some sort of shenanigans, but once Daisy arrived in Madison, there wasn't a peep from anyone back at Buttercup Lake, and I realized they just wanted Daisy to take this job.

It didn't help that Brielle had just broken up with me

for the millionth time but kept appearing at the bar to flirt with any man who looked at her.

I think she did it to make me jealous, but I realized it was a bad sign when it did the complete opposite, and I silently prayed for someone to sweep her off her feet.

Meanwhile, I stayed my distance from Daisy so Brielle wouldn't come unglued and cause a scene at the one place that brought me peace.

But the truth was that every single thought I had manifested Daisy.

Just like tonight.

I tried to ignore the similarities between myself and the giant green creature stomping around Whoville on my television.

Because I'd always loved Christmas.

Until recently.

Now, with all my brothers and cousins matched off, it had become a big reminder that I sucked at relationships as I sat alone in my vacation home, drinking rancid beer and wishing for a life that wasn't mine.

Even with Brielle. I knew we weren't a match, but so many people were against her that I thought I had to give her a shot… and another shot. I knew she wasn't exactly faithful, but I guess I didn't care enough to… care?

I let out a deep groan and smoothed my hands over my face to make it all disappear.

The drama of Brielle was enough to cure me of all relationships—past, present, and future.

And I didn't know what to make of having Daisy shoved onto me when I showed up at the community center.

It seemed suspicious, but I highly doubted Daisy was in on it.

My phone buzzed, and I saw my brother asking about the beer.

Shoot.

I tapped my finger on my knee and wondered what to say.

A little pucker never hurt anybody.

No. That wasn't right. Maybe...

It left a lingering effect on me.

No. I had to tell him the truth.

Possibly a little too much ginger? I'm unsure if it was just my bottle, but it seemed a little tart. Great effort, though.

I hit send and felt good about being honest while softening the delivery.

Maybe I didn't always have to be so direct.

His message came right over.

So, I have a shot of getting in your bar?

Well, so much for being less direct. I sighed, rubbed my eyes from exhaustion, and chuckled, picking up the phone again.

Just keep working on it, buddy. You'll get there.

He wrote back a question mark and smiley face. I let it go with a thumbs-up back and wondered if Daisy would be impressed with my gentle tact.

And there she went and slipped into my thoughts again.

It took me nearly a year to get her out of my head, and now, the Sunshine Breakfast Club had put her right back in.

It absolutely had to be them.

Right?

Or were they making me paranoid?

No. Yeah. No. It was all a coincidence.

I glanced at the clock and realized I hadn't eaten yet.

And Buttercup Lake Resort did have a fantastic

restaurant. And the bar Styx had great burgers and fries. I could totally justify some research to take back with me in a few days when I head south.

But did I need to justify anything?

So, what if I were a grown man going out into the blizzard to grab some food?

I stood and walked over to the fridge, opening it up to stare at the leftovers from last night. Chicken curry, rice, veggies… Grabbing the container, I opened the freezer and shoved it inside.

"Who doesn't love a good cheeseburger?" I muttered to myself.

A loud howl from down the hall made me jump. I'd had Purrlock Holmes for over a year and a half, and I still panicked when I heard his meow, yowl, or whatever the heck cats did.

"What is it now, Purrlock?" I hollered toward the pure white feline.

Purrlock was yet another memento from my relationship with Brielle. She begged for this kitty, and when she realized the brushing, changing litter, and vet appointments this living creature demanded, she lost interest.

And Purrlock and I had grown close since the breakup.

I realized she'd gotten stuck in the powder room as I followed the noise. She always liked to curl up on the heater vent next to the extra stack of towels.

I opened the door to see Purrlock with one blue eye and one hazel eye yowling at me as if it were my fault she got trapped. She curled between my legs, purring, and I bent down and scratched between her ears as she stood and arched her back.

"Good girl. I'm going to grab a burger and maybe bring you back some fish."

Her eyes widened, and she let out a little meow as she walked down the hall.

I washed my hands, ran my damp fingers through my hair, and glanced in the mirror.

"As good as it's gonna get."

But why did it matter?

It didn't.

I pulled on my jacket and wandered into the garage where the G wagon was parked. It was a great vehicle, but I was really at a point where I didn't want to keep being reminded of all my past relationship mistakes.

Maybe I'd trade it in. Start afresh for the new year.

As the garage door opened, I got into my car and started it up. Pulling out of the garage, I took a deep breath when the snowflakes hit the windshield. The meteorologists were right about tonight's snowstorm.

By the time I followed the road into town, an inch had stuck to the pavement, and the soft light of the resort glowed in the distance. The small downtown area along the lakefront still had a couple of cars parked along the street while the café and coffee shop served the few people courageous enough to brave the storm.

Oversized red bows hung on the lampposts wound with green garland. It was good to be back in Buttercup Lake, even if only for a day or two. This little town always knew how to do the holidays right. Since I'd moved to Madison, I missed that small-town charm.

And my family, but I'd never let them know that.

I slowly turned onto the road to the resort and gripped the wheel as the flakes became larger. The parking lot was packed for it being midweek, but then flickering lights caught my eye. My pulse pounded as emergency vehicles came into view. Red and white flashing lights from two of the town's fire trucks bounced off the main resort building, and I spotted a group of people congregating near the restaurant's entrance.

My gaze landed on a woman wrapped in a blanket, talking to the fire chief, and my heart hammered in my chest.

Daisy!

25

Was it Daisy?

I quickly turned into the parking lot and parked in the nearest spot, away from the emergency vehicles but close to the hotel.

It felt like the world stood still as I jumped out of my SUV and barreled through the small crowd.

A large fire hose snaked into the restaurant's front door, and Nate stepped forward to slow me down. He was the local sheriff and only a few years older than me.

"Whoa. Everything's fine." He held his hand up and laughed. "Are you looking for your takeout order or something?"

I scowled and shook my head, scanning where I thought I saw Daisy. "No, I just thought I saw someone I knew. What happened?"

"Small kitchen fire. Mostly smoke damage, but I estimate the bar will be closed for a few weeks."

"Nobody hurt?" I asked, glancing toward an ambulance with the back doors wide open.

"Everybody got out just fine." He eyed me suspiciously. That was one of the problems growing up in a small town like Buttercup Lake. Nate not only happened to be the sheriff, but he was great friends with my older brothers, Cash and Beckett. They'd all grown up together and loved to pick on the youngest kid.

Me.

Nate rocked back on his heels. "We've got things handled here. You can probably go back home."

I chuckled, not moving. "I just need to find someone."

Nate's brow arched as some hotel staff led the small group toward the lobby after the fire chief gave the all-clear.

"Who?" he asked, tilting his head.

I shrugged. "Does it matter?"

Nate chuckled and shook his head. "Not particularly, but I thought I might know the answer."

That was the other problem about growing up around here. I was hyper-defensive because I was the younger brother that everyone picked on.

"Daisy. I'm looking for Daisy."

Nate nodded. "Some guy in a Camaro picked her up about two minutes ago."

My stomach dropped. "Oh."

Nate laughed and shook his head. "Kidding. But man, you should have seen your expression."

"Seriously?" I glared at him, reminding myself that he was now someone who could put me in jail for the holidays. And he'd probably do it just for giggles with my brothers.

27

"Calm down. Geesh. She's in the ambulance getting checked out for smoke inhalation."

My heart rate jumped. "I thought you said nobody was hurt."

His hand went up. "Just a precaution. Since when have you two been buddies, anyway?"

"She worked for me down in Madison."

Nate nodded slowly and smoothed his hand over his jaw. "Oh, yeah. That's right. She told us all about that."

I frowned. "Who's us?"

"Oh, just me and the guys at the station. She drops off fudge and cookies on the regular."

"Really?"

"Sweet girl."

"She's not a girl. She's a woman." I nodded. "But yeah, she's very nice."

Nate nodded. "Alright. Well, if I bump into her, I'll let her—"

"No need." I pushed past him.

"Well, that's my sign to go home and crack open a bottle of gingerbread beer your brother left at my house earlier."

I stopped and turned around. "Oh, yeah."

Nate nodded. "Been waiting all day to get a little

festive."

I laughed, knowing he was in for a treat. "You enjoy that beer now, Nate."

"I plan on it."

Realizing I wasn't the better person, I made my way to the ambulance, where I instantly heard her laughter ring through the air.

It was like my drug.

The moment I heard the melody, I wanted more and more.

I poked my head around the opening, and my eyes landed on her, huddled under the blanket with an oxygen mask.

"Daisy." I hadn't meant to say her name aloud.

Her brows furrowed, and her head tilted. "Hunter?"

Her voice was muffled from the mask. "What are you doing here?"

"I wanted a cheeseburger."

"Oh, well. I don't think that's happening tonight."

The medic checked the oximeter on her index finger and removed the mask.

"Are you still feeling okay?" the medic asked.

"Totally fine. I swear." She nodded, smiling.

Dang, I missed seeing her smile.

The medic nodded. "Alright. If you experience any of the symptoms we spoke about, go straight to the emergency room."

"Will do. Thanks, Lacy." Daisy kept the blanket wrapped around her shoulders and started toward the opening of the ambulance.

I offered my hand to help her down, and she grinned. "Chivalry twice in one night?"

"What can I say?"

Daisy smiled as a snowflake landed on her nose. "It's really coming down now."

"It is." I shoved my hands in my pockets. "Hey, did you need a ride home?"

Daisy shook her head. "Thanks for the offer, but Millie is coming to pick me up. She said she was finishing up some shopping at the antique store down the street."

A diesel truck rumbled behind me, and I spun around to see Millie in the driver's seat. She looked extremely surprised to see me.

"Ah, right on time," I muttered.

Millie rolled down her window and smiled. "Hunter, what are you doing here?"

"Came for a burger, but I guess I'm out of luck."

Daisy started toward the truck, and I followed close

behind.

"Oh, Daisy." Millie puckered her lips into a frown. "I bought a little more than I expected at the shop. You know, a little Christmas shopping for my Jackson. There's really no place for you to sit comfortably."

Daisy pulled her blanket tighter, and I glanced into the passenger seat, where a bag the size of a shoebox had been left.

That was it?

"Hunter, would you be a dear and drop Daisy off at her house? She's just down the road from you."

"Are—" I started to ask Millie the obvious, but she gave me the death stare before peeling out of the snowy parking lot.

Daisy turned and let out a sigh, shivering. "I'm starting to get the distinct feeling that Sunshine Breakfast Club is up to something."

I pulled off my jacket and draped it over Daisy's shoulders since the blanket wasn't doing the trick.

I grinned. "What makes you think that?"

"Just a hunch." Daisy shook her head and chuckled.

"Okay. So, let's get you home before the blizzard hits."

Daisy nodded and glanced at me. "You really don't

31

have to do this. I'm sure I can get my boss to take me home."

"I am not disobeying Millie. Besides, I have to prove to you that I'm not a jerk."

She laughed, following me to my SUV. "I don't think you are, but I might take back my opinion on your heated seats in a few seconds. My boss said my coat was a total loss, and I'm freezing." Daisy glanced at me. "And your car is already running. Maybe your girlfriend knew what she was talking about."

"Ex," I clarified.

I opened the passenger door for her, and she nearly fell into the seat with a shiver. "And the heater is full blast. Freaking awesome."

I laughed, closing the door and walking to my side.

"Are you coming around to the seats?" I asked, sliding in.

Daisy's big hazel eyes landed on mine, and a thrill ran through me. There was something about being so close to her that just lit up my world.

She chuckled and shook her head. "No. I still can't get over that creeping sensation."

I nodded in agreement and turned out of the parking lot. "I didn't know you lived near me."

"Well, I'm not on the lakeside. I'm across the street

from the lake," she said, turning to look at me. "But I'm only about four houses down, I think?"

"We could have carpooled to Madison."

"Yeah, I'm sure your girlfriend would have loved that. She seemed a little possessive."

I chuckled. "Again, my ex, and yeah. I don't think she really wanted me. She just didn't want anyone else to have me either."

Daisy laughed and shook her head. "Ugh. Relationships are so complicated. Count me out."

Chapter Three

Daisy

I didn't know which was worse, that I was out of a job and paycheck for the next couple of weeks, or that I had to ride in Hunter's car for the second time in one night and act like I wasn't ready to explode. It was like the man's aura just pulled me into his world.

And that world wasn't where I wanted to be.

I wasn't into fancy cars, bling, and city living. I loved small towns, stuffing my Subaru with camping equipment, and getting away from it all.

Hunter obviously liked the opposite of all that, judging by his ex and his car.

I was pretty certain Brielle had lashes for her lashes, whereas I couldn't even get the mascara to stay on my actual lashes.

Not to mention her clothes. They were always beautiful, albeit over the top for some celebrations. I chuckled, thinking back to when she took a tumble down the hill a year before at the apple orchard. Had she not been wearing six-inch heels disguised as boots, she might have made it down the hill, but what I remembered most was the way she treated Hunter when he came to her rescue. She took it all out on him, and by the time Millie had mentioned me working down for him in Madison, I think Brielle was ready to thump him.

So, to say that I was ecstatic to get home last night and put on my flannels would be an understatement. Not only did I need to thaw out, but I also needed to forget about Hunter.

Except that I couldn't.

He'd mentioned he was headed back down to Madison in a couple of days, and I'd say the sooner, the better.

But I did owe him a batch of fudge before he left town.

One thing I didn't like to do was go back on my word. A deal was a deal.

Christmas music rang through the air as I stared at the

fudge, hoping it would set before the next snowstorm made its way here. Foxy was still on the outs, but she'd been towed to my driveway this morning, so I wanted to be able to walk over to Hunter's house to deliver the fudge.

I glanced out my kitchen window and noticed two deer in my front yard, nosing the flakes from the night before. Giddiness washed over me as they lifted their heads and glanced in my direction. It didn't matter that deer, fox, and turkey made my front yard their superhighway. I still got as excited about seeing them now as when I first moved here a little over a year and a half ago. I noticed the house across the street from me on the lakeside no longer had the *For Sale* sign out.

I sure hoped the new neighbors would be nice, whoever they were. There were times when I missed Silver Ridge back in Washington, but I'd needed a fresh start, and moving to be closer to the family I had left was perfect.

Both deer turned to look toward my driveway and bounded away. I quickly made my way to the front door and peered out the tiny window to see Millie marching up my sidewalk. Her eyes sparkled when they connected with mine. I noticed a small package in her hand and smiled.

"I see you made it home safely last night," Millie said, waggling her silver brows as she made her way to my porch.

"Any overnight visitors inside?"

"Millie, I can't believe you asked that."

"What? It's no secret you're a flirt, or at the very least, a talker."

I scowled. "I did not sleep with Hunter Knox. Flirting is one thing. Being naked in the same bed is quite another. Besides, I haven't flirted with him either."

"What? No flirting? I wouldn't blame you for wiggling your hips around him a little. Hunter's a good-looking man, and it's the holidays. Who doesn't need a jolly old time?" Her eyes still twinkled with mischief. "You young ones are far too reclusive."

I laughed, inviting her inside and shaking my head. "I'm not reclusive, Millie. I work at a bar and chat with people for hours a day. I volunteer at the animal shelter, and I even come to the Sunshine Breakfast Club when time allows. Speaking of, you've sent me on more matchmaking errands than I can even keep track of, and now I'm worried it's payback." I shut the door behind her.

"Speaking of, here's the book we started. You need to get chapters one through eight read by next week." She shoved a package in my hand.

I eyed the festively wrapped rectangle and smiled. I should have known I wasn't getting off that easily.

Millie took a deep breath and closed her eyes. "Smells like chocolate." She glanced at my kitchen counter, and her brows rose. "Just made some fudge, I see?"

"I did."

"And you're not offering me any," she said, patting my hands, still clutching the book. "So, who's the fudge for?"

My cheeks reddened. "Hunter. You know, since he gave me a ride."

Just saying his name gave me the butterflies. Just in the two times I'd spent with him last night, he'd seemed so… different. Friendly, even? I shook those thoughts right out of my head.

"Oh, right. Of course." Her high-pitched giggle competed with *Sleigh Bells* floating through my stereo.

"Strictly platonic, Millie. Don't think I'm not onto you." I could not give her or the other members any ammunition or they'd make the holidays a living, eating, breathing, matchmaking event. I'd been on the other side of this before. I knew what they were capable of.

I stared at Millie, not giving her the upper hand. "I just needed to get it to him before he goes back down to Madison."

"Uh-huh." Millie winked at me. "Well, I'd better be off. Jackson is waiting for me at the house, but I told him I'd bring him back a peppermint mocha."

She wandered toward the door and opened it before turning around to look at me. "And Daisy, he is a really good guy who's just had really bad luck with the women he chooses."

I chuckled nervously. "I didn't say anything."

"You never would. Now, go put on that cute fuzzy sweater that hits your midriff and maybe those stonewashed jeans you have. His SUV is in the driveway, so I'm sure he's home." Before I had a chance to say a word, she closed the door, leaving me to contemplate my life's decisions.

I watched the woman, nearly sixty years my senior, waddling down my walkway as if this was what she did every day of her life.

And come to think of it, maybe it was.

I glanced down at my flannel pajamas and scowled. Obviously, I wasn't going to show up to Hunter's in my flannel pajamas.

But I certainly hadn't given any thought to what I was going to wear for the day.

Did it really matter?

I let out a groan.

This had to be why I was still single.

I was clueless.

39

No, I was single because I chose to be.

Maybe Millie was right, though. I could wear that sweater and just button up my coat so I didn't freeze to death on the walk over to his house.

No, this was ridiculous. I was merely dropping off some fudge for a guy who'd done a favor for me.

The fudge would be set in about twenty minutes, which would give me plenty of time to shower.

Nerves flared through me unexpectedly, and I let out a huff of annoyance. Before Millie showed up, I'd planned on putting on a pair of sweats, delivering the fudge, and coming back home to decorate for Christmas.

Instead, she planted a little seed of something that I couldn't shake.

Maybe it should matter what I wore to see him.

But why would it?

"Argh." I stomped my foot and let out a chuckle as I made my way to my bedroom.

I ignored my closet, walked into my bathroom, and turned on the shower.

I was *not* going to be swayed by Millie or any other member of the Sunshine Breakfast Club. I was onto them.

All of them.

In fact, by the time I got out of the shower, dressed in

the midriff sweater, grabbed the fudge, and trudged my way over to Hunter's, I was steamed.

I had enough going on in my life. I was fulfilled.

Besides, I'd loved before, and it hurt more than anything to lose them. I certainly didn't need to go repeating that pattern.

Flirting with everyone was better than dating anyone.

As I rang Hunter's doorbell, I tapped my boot impatiently while waiting for him to open the door.

My naked Christmas tree needed me.

"Daisy, hey." His blue eyes fastened on mine the moment he opened the door, and every traitor of a cell I had in my body ignited as if I'd never seen a sexy man before.

"Here's your fudge." I shoved the plate into his hands. "Merry Christmas."

I turned around to head back home, but his hand gently gripped my arm. "It's too cold to walk home. Let me drive you."

"Absolutely not. I don't need your fancy seats. I'm just fine." I glanced over my shoulder to see him staring at me with a mischievous glint in his eye. "But thanks for the offer."

Without warning, a willowy white cat snaked between Hunter's legs, and he gasped. "No, Purrlock Holmes. Stay." He handed me the plate back and dove for the cat, who

41

hissed at him as he landed in the snow next to her. She curled her tail and meowed as Hunter scooped the cat into his arms and stood.

"Did you just call her Purrlock Holmes?" My brows rose. "Because I'm pretty sure you did."

He turned around and dropped Purrlock into his house before quickly shutting the door.

"She's an escape artist."

I laughed. "Not a detective?"

His smile reached his eyes as he took the plate of fudge from me, unwrapped the plastic wrap, and snuck a piece of fudge. "I should have named her Purrdini."

"Look at you go with the puns and stuff."

He popped the entire piece of fudge in his mouth. "Mmm. Dang. How did you make this so creamy?"

I grinned and shrugged, opening up my jacket to reveal the sweater Millie had told me to wear.

His gaze swept across my bare midriff, and a smile edged its way deeper into his gaze.

Maybe Millie was onto something.

"A family recipe used by millions. I use marshmallow crème." I folded my arms across my chest and watched Hunter reach under the plastic wrap for another piece. "And for the record, how can you possibly make fun of Foxy when you named your cat Purrlock?"

He cocked his head. "What do you mean?"

"Seriously? You think Purrlock Holmes is a normal cat name?"

Hunter chuckled. "It's a cat. You named an inanimate object something sexy and provocative."

"My Subaru turned you on? Is that what you're saying?"

The look in his eyes stirred something deep inside me.

There was something so familiar and comforting behind his eyes.

I dropped my gaze and cleared my throat. "Anyway, I need to get back. I have big plans for the afternoon."

"Oh, yeah?" He wrapped the plastic wrap over the plate. "What are they?"

"I'm decorating my tree."

"Nice. Sounds fun." He nodded, turned around, and opened the door, sliding the plate of fudge on a table in his foyer. In an instant, his coat was in his hands. "I think that sounds like the perfect afternoon."

"Yeah. Me too."

He shut the door and locked it.

My brows raised. "Where are you going?"

Hunter laughed and took a deep breath. "To help you

decorate."

"Don't you need an invite for that?"

"You did invite me." He smiled, sending a tingly current clear to my toes.

"No, I didn't."

"You don't have to be rude about it." His smile widened. "But you did."

"I'd remember if I invited you, and I did not."

"That's not what I remember." He draped his arm over my shoulders.

"Fine. You clearly need some form of entertainment today, and I'll gladly oblige if this wipes the slate clean."

"What slate?"

I laughed, shaking my head. "You're driving me crazy."

"Crazy good or crazy bad?"

I shook my head. "I don't know."

But I liked it and would never admit that to him or anyone else on this planet.

"I'm only giving you a hard time."

I laughed, shoving my hands into my coat. "You really didn't have to explain that part to me. I got it. Loud and clear."

"In all seriousness, I'm super handy. I can wrap lights

around a tree like nobody else, and I can reach the top of eighty percent of Christmas trees to put the star on top."

"I have an angel."

"Yes, you are."

"Yes, I am what?"

"An angel."

I stomped my foot. "What the heck is going on with you? Did you pour too much Baileys in your coffee? Add too much Schnapps to your eggnog?"

"It's noon."

"You're telling me you never tipple a little before the afternoon."

He grinned. "I own a bar. I don't think that would be a great idea. In fact, I think it might be a sign that I need help."

I chuckled, feeling the familiar tingle pepper through me. "Okay, fine. Let's just get going."

"Honestly, I think we should drive."

"Fine. If you want Cruella's hot seats, we'll drive."

Hunter frowned, unlocking the car. "Cruella?"

"Yeah. That's what I named her."

"You named my car?"

I nodded. "It seemed fitting."

Chapter Four

Hunter

I followed Daisy into her home, and the sweet smells of chocolate and vanilla filled the air. Her tidy kitchen was decorated with Santa towels hanging on the fridge, candy cane potholders dangling from the cabinets, and a ceramic Christmas tree on the tiny island.

Her tree stood bare in the corner of her living room, which was perfectly Daisy. A red throw had been tossed over her white couch. A series of black and white photos of puppies hung over the brick fireplace. A rattan lamp lit up the opposite corner from the tree where a rocking chair had been tucked. The coffee table had a spread of catalogs displayed, the top one being a local cheese catalog.

She turned to face me, tugging her jacket off. "What?"

"It's just fun to see where you live."

Daisy grunted and held out her hand to take my coat. She made her way to a tiny closet and hung our jackets.

"I don't know why that would be." She shrugged. "It's not like I have two heads. I'm just a normal woman, trying to keep things together."

I shook my head, laughing. "There's nothing normal about you, Daisy."

I wanted to add that she was extraordinary.

If someone could hold magic at their fingertips, Daisy's magic would be her ability to turn anyone's bad day into a good day. I saw it time and again in my bar.

And anyone who had a series of puppy photos obviously didn't hold much bitterness inside.

She cast me a funny look as a piece of hair fell from her loose braid. She was the most beautiful woman I'd ever seen. Every night at the bar, I thought that, and here it happened again.

But ever since Millie stopped by this morning telling me to be funnier and more laid back around Daisy, I couldn't stop myself from treating her like one of my brothers. The only difference at this point was that she didn't have a beard.

And I honestly couldn't figure out why I was listening to Millie at all. There wasn't a reason in the world Daisy would be interested in me. And I still didn't understand why Millie appeared on my doorstep other than to give me a peppermint mocha that had the name *Jackson* scrawled on it.

I walked over to the tree and traced one of the limbs. The fresh smell of fir escaped into the air, and I spun around to look at Daisy. She was just so natural. There was nothing over the top about her.

Even today, she was in a sexy pair of slouchy jeans and a cropped sweater. It was perfectly Daisy.

"This tree smells so good." I sniffed. "Incredible."

"What has gotten into you?" Her eyes narrowed on me. "You're all chipper and stuff. It's like I'm watching a chipmunk on speed. You're caressing my tree, falling in love with my Subaru... I'm used to you sulking in a corner of your bar. Not this."

"I wasn't sulking." I walked closer to Daisy. "I just had a lot on my mind."

"And now?" She chuckled. "Did everything just go *poof* in there?"

"Hardly. It's just good to be back in Buttercup Lake." I rubbed my hands together. "So, what can I do to help?"

She reached for a remote and turned on her stereo, piping Christmas carols through the air.

"I'll be right back." She gave me another funny look before walking out of the room, and I realized I'd better cool it.

Just because Millie mentioned to lighten up didn't mean I had to act like an idiot. Although, it wasn't a stretch, and it felt pretty natural. Daisy just made me… happy.

But I didn't realize she thought I'd been sulking in the corner last year when she worked for me.

Daisy reappeared, holding a red and green plastic box.

"Let me help." I rushed toward her, and she shook her head.

"I got it, but you can go get the other one. It's down the hall in the room that's the second door on your right."

I quickly made my way down the hall and into a room that looked like a guest room. A full-size bed with a snowflake quilt was near a window, and a small writing desk sat next to it. I spotted a red and green box in front of the closet and hoisted it up when I noticed a small picture frame with Daisy hugging a guy who looked about the same age as her in the photo. Maybe late teens at the time? She looked incredibly happy and like she didn't have a care in the world.

As I hauled the box out to the living room, Daisy was

rifling through the other one, pulling out clumps of lights.

"Oh, how I missed you," she squealed, and I looked over to see what she was squeezing.

"What in the world is that thing?"

She grinned as her eyes twinkled. "This, my friend, is my naughty Christmas gnome."

I chuckled. "Is she as frisky as Foxy?"

Her eyes widened, and a pink flushed her cheek. "More." She let out a happy sigh. "I just love Christmas."

"I'm stunned." I stared at her before putting my box down.

"Why's that?" She frowned, scratching her head. Her hazel eyes landed on mine, and a smile crept onto her face.

"Your place is so tidy, and you just remind me of someone who would wind up their lights, not toss them in the box all tangled."

She laughed and shrugged. "I'm just full of surprises. Stick around long enough, and you might see how I organize my spatulas."

I shook my head, laughing as she sat on the floor and started untangling the lights.

"What brought you up here?" she asked, looking at me between unknotting the green string. "Isn't it a pretty busy time? It was last year."

I nodded, taking a seat on the floor next to her. "Yeah, it's pretty nuts, but I hired a manager who is doing a great job of keeping order."

She nodded and slid the first untangled string toward me. "That's good. It always looked like you were overworking yourself."

I hid a smile, wondering how often she'd noticed me while I was pretending not to notice her.

"Yeah. I'm getting better at taking breaks, and my brother Cash wanted me to come up and help him with some stuff."

"That's nice of you."

I stood with the first string of lights in my hand. "Mind if I check them first? Where's a good plug?"

"Nah. I just got them last year. Go for it."

"You sure?"

Daisy nodded, and I, despite my best judgment, started wrapping the lights around the tree.

As Daisy worked on the next string of lights, she hummed softly and swayed her body. I'd been such a fool last year, keeping my distance the way I had.

She stood and handed me the next string as I made my way around the tree.

"When are you headed back to Madison?"

"Oh, tomorrow or the next day. Just depends."

She eyed me, stepping closer. "On what?"

"Whether Cash still needs my help."

She nodded and let out a wistful sigh. "I have a confession."

"You're falling madly in love with me?"

She laughed, rolling her eyes. "No, but I might have been wrong about you."

I smiled to myself as she handed me the third string of lights she had untangled. "How so?"

"You're not as much of a grump as I thought."

I laughed, nodding. "Progress. I'll take it. I have a confession, too."

Her eyes lit up. "You're going to steal Foxy from me in the middle of the night?"

"Hardly." I turned to look at Daisy bending over the box in the coziness of her home, and I couldn't help but feel a pang of longing. It felt so... easy around her, even when I'd invited myself over to help decorate her tree.

But why wouldn't it? I was just an acquaintance helping her out with something.

"Spill it. What do you have to confess to me? You're married with a family?"

"Boy, you really do have the bar set low," I teased as

she handed me the last string. Her hands brushed against mine, and a current ran through us. She looked away, and I knew she'd felt it, too. "My confession is that Millie stopped by my house this morning and told me to lighten up around you."

Her brows knitted together with a smirk. "Yeah?"

"So, I've been picturing you as one of my brothers sans the beard."

Daisy laughed, and it was the best sound in the world.

"We should probably stop talking and unpack what that really means, but I can't help but think the Sunshine Breakfast Club has set its sights on us."

I laughed.

"Well, Millie stopped by before I delivered your fudge."

"Really?"

I nodded. "And she gave me a piece of advice, too."

"Which was what?"

She blushed and tugged on her sweater, but it didn't budge. "She told me to wear this sweater."

I grinned, nodding. "Well, she wasn't wrong. You look sensational."

Her gaze lifted to mine. "You think?"

"Yeah. Although I'm pretty sure you could put a bag over your body and still look like someone I'd want to…" I stopped, and her eyes flashed to mine with a glimmer.

"Someone you'd…?" she continued.

I laughed. "Nothing."

She wandered over to the opened box and pulled out a tray of ornaments.

"I really don't know what Millie is thinking," she said. "We are not a match."

My heart sank. "How do you figure?"

She snickered and hung a glittery snowflake on a branch.

"No offense, but I've seen your type."

I scowled and shook my head. "Brielle is not my type."

"Then why were you with her?"

"It's complicated."

"How so?"

I reached for a glass Santa ornament and stared at it. "I felt bad for her. My parents and brothers were against Brielle. And I honestly just kept thinking there had to be substance deep down inside her."

Daisy studied me silently, and my heart raced as she analyzed what I'd just said.

Great.

I totally sounded like a jerk.

Again.

"Are you saying she was shallow?" Daisy finally asked.

I wandered back to the ornament box and lifted a sparkly snowman out.

"We just didn't connect. I couldn't peel back any layers, and the longer I was with her, the more I realized that. She liked that she was dating the owner of a popular bar."

Daisy nodded and hung a glass icicle. "But she seemed pretty protective around you. How did she take it?"

"The breakup?"

Daisy nodded.

"Not great at first, but I think that's because when she broke it off and wanted to get back together again for the millionth time, she expected me to take her back again. I don't think it had anything to do with me as a person. I think she just liked calling the shots, but…" I debated how much to say. I looked over at Daisy, who was clinging to every word. "She wasn't faithful."

Her hands slid to her mouth, and she gasped. "I'm so sorry."

I shrugged, realizing I never felt the emotions I should have felt when I found out about Brielle. But that was another reason I knew there was no repairing anything.

"So, she broke up with you, but you didn't take her back?"

"Yeah."

"Hmm. Interesting." She wandered to her kitchen and opened the fridge. "Would you like a soda or a beer?"

I glanced at the microwave clock. "Well, it is past noon, so I'll take a beer."

She chuckled and grabbed two. "Good choice. If we're going to dig deep into your dating life, we'll need this liquid courage."

"Whoa." My hands shot up in the air. "My dating life? Why would we need to go there at all?"

"Why not?" She chuckled. "I don't have one, and yours sounds fascinating, complex, and impossible to unwrap."

"Honestly, it's not that complicated."

She handed me a beer. "You didn't break things off with her. She broke them off with you."

"But I didn't take her back," I pointed out, clanking my beer to hers. "Cheers."

"Cheers." She shook her head and took a swig. "But it didn't sound like you were into her, yet you didn't end things on your terms."

Daisy's lips pressed against the tip of the bottle, and I

couldn't help my mind from going to places it shouldn't.

"Are you saying I'm a chicken?"

She winked at me, and my chest squeezed unexpectedly.

"Bock. Bock."

I laughed, glancing around her home. There was something special about it.

She looked out the window, and her eyes met mine. "The snow is coming down really hard now."

Daisy walked over to the fireplace and switched it on while I picked up a glass ball ornament.

"It's kind of nice to have someone help decorate the tree." She watched me closely, but I didn't know what to say. I'd pushed my way into this event all because Millie had mentioned that the holidays were hard for Daisy. She didn't elaborate, but here I was.

"I'm glad you let me force my way into your home without calling the police."

She chuckled and took a sip of her beer. "I'm not sure whose side Nate would be on, to be honest." She pushed her lips into a sexy pout. "Especially if the Sunshine Breakfast Club is in on this."

I cocked my head slightly. "This?"

"You know… pushing us together."

Christmas of Love

"You sure that's what's going on?"

She didn't answer but sat down on the couch, pulling a pillow over her lap to prop her elbows and beer on top of it.

I set my bottle down and grabbed a tray of silver balls for the tree. "Well, Nate is more my brothers' friend. If there were ever a guy to stuff another guy into a locker back in high school, it would have been him."

My eyes widened. "Our sheriff?"

He nodded. "I mean, he never did it, but I know stories that would blow your mind. He was known as the practical joker of the school."

"Wow. I never would have guessed."

She pulled her legs underneath her and stretched toward the ceiling. "But he never stuffed you into one, right?"

I grinned. "No."

"That's good." She smiled and let out a sigh. "I bet you were a jock in high school, and all the cheerleaders wanted you."

I nearly choked on my beer at her assumption. "Yeah? Where'd you come up with that?"

"Just how you carry yourself."

I laughed and shook my head, hanging another ornament. "Great. So, I carry myself like a guy stuck in high school."

She giggled, and the sound was addicting. "No, but you just seem... confident. So, am I right?"

"I wasn't a football guy, but I did play soccer and baseball."

She waggled her finger. "I knew it."

"How about you? What were you like in high school?"

A shadow drifted over Daisy's expression, and she cleared her throat, shrugging. "Just a normal teenager."

Her eyes wouldn't meet mine, and I knew that was all she was going to tell me.

Chapter Five

Daisy

Grief was unpredictable. That was the only predictable thing about it. I glanced at my empty beer bottle, and my belly growled.

"Hungry?" My eyes met Hunter's, and relief spread through his gaze.

I must not have done as good of a job as I thought, trying to play off how I truly felt about high school. Actually, high school had been fine. It was the last bit of normalcy I had until everything in my life came to a stop.

Darn. I had to work on that.

"I'd love something to eat. How can I help?" he

asked, setting the tray of ornaments down.

"If you're good at opening cardboard packaging, have at it. I've got some great freezer snacks we can tear into." I hopped off the couch and walked into the kitchen.

Hunter followed me to the fridge, leaning over my shoulder. The warmth of his breath skating along my scalp sent a wave of goosebumps over me.

The good kind.

"Anyway, I've got some pizza bites, fried ravioli, spanakopita, and taquitos."

He laughed, his low, sexy growl of a sound, and I closed my eyes for a second. Whenever I heard that back at the bar, it stopped me in my tracks.

There was something so manly and sexy and... Hunter... about it.

I blinked my eyes open, pulled out the boxes, and shut the door with my foot, all without bumping into Hunter.

Mariah Carey came singing on the stereo, and I tried to pretend her words didn't hit him.

Hunter wouldn't be so bad for Christmas.

A one and done type of thing.

No commitments.

Just unwrap him.

Enjoy myself.

And put a bow on him before I send him back into the world.

I slid the box of taquitos over to him onto the counter.

"You open that one. I always have a hard time ripping the plastic."

Hunter's eyes met mine, and another thrill of something unexpected shot through me.

"You know, there's these handy things called scissors nowadays."

I chuckled. "Fine. You just got a glimpse into how lazy I can be when I'm hungry."

Hunter's gaze stayed on mine. "Daisy, I've seen how you work. There is one word I would never call you, and it's lazy."

A little sprout of surprise grew in my belly. "You actually noticed me at your bar?"

He locked both arms on the counter and stared at me. "Daisy, I more than noticed you. I had to do everything in my power to pretend you didn't exist."

His words fluttered and flapped through me like a spastic cardinal trying to get my attention.

I opened the fried ravioli and took a breath.

"Are you just saying that because you're one beer into this afternoon?"

Hunter laughed and shook his head. "It takes more than a beer for me to start saying things I don't mean."

I bent down to grab the cookie sheet and regroup.

What was going on?

He didn't utter two sentences to me last year, and now...

It was the club. Millie must have planted some crazy idea in Hunter's head, and it was my job to get it out.

I straightened and slid the tray in front of us.

"Well, anyway. Let's get these snacks cooking, shall we?"

Hunter laughed and nodded, dumping some taquitos on his side.

But this was kind of a great opening to hear more about Hunter's old relationship. I'd seen enough of it to be very confused by the whole thing.

"Right. We got off track earlier."

His brow arched, and a few deep wrinkles ran along his forehead. "We did?"

I nodded, arranging the snacks on the tray as the oven warmed. "Yeah. I wanted to dissect your relationship."

"Ah, man. I thought you'd somehow managed to forget that."

"Nope. I have a memory as good as an elephant. Some

might even say a dolphin."

He chuckled. "Ooh, a dolphin. I'd better watch what I say. I wouldn't want something coming up to haunt me in a few years."

My stomach roiled with excited uncertainty. Would we still be talking in a few years?

No. Don't jump ahead like that, Daisy. Get a grip. The beer' was doing the talking.

I turned around to the fridge and opened the door. "Want another beer?"

"I guess I could always walk home. What the heck? Sure."

My feet did a little happy dance as I pulled both beers out, pushing one into his hand. I was enjoying Hunter's company far more than I realized.

The oven beeped, and I shoved the tray of food inside.

"We established that you were a chicken," I joked. "But why?"

He smoothed his hand along his chest and chuckled. "I didn't know we'd agreed to that about me."

I leaned against my small island, taking in Hunter. There was no doubt about it. Every drop of the guy was gorgeous. Even his faults were flattering. Well, I guess to most, they wouldn't be faults, but I generally dated lanky guys, and Hunter was all muscle.

Thick muscles.

Hunter's brows pulled together. "You're blushing."

I frowned, laughing. "No, I'm not."

"You are."

"I'm not." I gathered a couple of plates. "So, you had the case of the bock- bocks."

"Pardon?" He laughed, tipping the bottle back. "Oh, I get it. Bock bock Chicken."

"But what was the real reason? You said you didn't want to hurt her feelings, but what about your feelings? I find it suspicious. You're a strong man. You run one of the most successful bars in all of Madison. And you were worried to break up with her? I don't buy it."

"I'm holding a deep, dark secret that I didn't want anyone to know."

"Yeah? Give it to me."

"I'm a genuinely nice guy."

I rolled my eyes and chuckled. "So nice that you couldn't even have a decent convo with me last year."

"I told you why."

I shook my head. "I don't know."

He let out a tortured grunt as Eartha Kitt's *Santa Baby* rang through the air. "Fine. My brothers have found their

65

one." Hunter did air quotes. "And I wanted to believe deep in my heart that I was next. I don't like coming home to an empty place. I want kids. I want to grow old with someone like my parents."

Hunter's eyes met mine, and electricity zipped through me. His gaze dropped to my lips before he turned away. "So, I was willing to overlook a few problems if it meant I could have the life I'd always wanted."

It felt like a ton of bricks had been dropped on me. "You want to settle down that badly?"

He turned back around and let out a deep breath. "Yeah. Truth is, I'm not even sure I want to be in Madison anymore. It's partly why I got a new manager for down there." His eyes stayed on mine, and a shot of something surprising swam through me.

Empathy for Hunter.

I just always assumed he was some player who wanted a glitzy girlfriend for when it suited him.

Hunter ran his fingers through his dark hair. "I also didn't want to hurt her feelings. She seemed so confused, and there were days where I think she really did love me and other days where she was just confused and distracted."

"And by distracted, you mean… with other men."

Hunter grinned. "I think she had a bad case of the

grassisgreeneritis."

I frowned and scooted closer to him. "The grassisgreeneritis? What's that?"

He chuckled. "The grass is greener."

I laughed, shaking my head. "Oh, my word. How did I not pick up on that?"

The oven timer dinged, and I grabbed a candy cane potholder. "You're telling me there's not some deep, dark secret about why you haven't found the right person?"

I grabbed the hot tray and put it on a snowflake trivet on the island.

"Or why you stuck it out with the wrong one?" I corrected.

"I don't know. I'm sure a psychologist would have a field day with me, but I don't know. Maybe two years ago, I was still trying to impress people. I got the fancy car, a splashy apartment…" He shrugged as I handed him the first plate.

"You're saying you've grown?"

"Maybe a little." He flashed me a boyish grin.

I nodded. "Brielle is gorgeous. No doubt there."

"So are you," he said softly. "You're actually my type."

The compliment took me off-guard. My cheeks warmed, and I looked at the tray of food.

67

"What do you mean, your type?" I asked, genuinely curious.

He took a fried ravioli from the tray and popped it in his mouth as he looked around my house. "This is what I love."

"Christmas décor?"

Hunter laughed, shaking his head. "Your home is so inviting and warm. You should see my apartment back in Madison. It's so sleek and cold and…"

"You didn't decorate?"

He shook his head. "You know what it is?"

"I honestly don't."

"It's like I checked out of my own life two years ago when things started taking off for me. I didn't know what to do with all the success."

"I could see that."

"Anyway, I want a home. I want a family." Hunter let out a blissful sigh. "But I'm not going to force anything ever again. If it happens, it happens."

I nodded in agreement. "I'm more of a serial flirter and less of a relationship person."

"Tell me." He smiled, and I felt my belly knot into a tangle of lust. "When was the last relationship you've had?"

That was definitely what this had to be.

"You won't believe me." I reached for a taquito and took a bite.

"Try me."

"I've never been in one."

"Hold on. You wanted to dissect my relationship, and you haven't been in one? Ever?"

I chuckled. "It gives me a unique perspective. Anyway, it's better that way. I like to have my freedom. If I want to pack up Foxy and head to the woods, I can. If I want to stay in on a Friday night and read a good book, no one stops me."

Hunter nodded, tapping his finger on the counter. "What if you found someone who loaded Foxy up for camping for you or read alongside with you?"

The energy in the room shifted as I randomly saw a vision of my future.

And it included Hunter.

I blinked my eyes and let out a shaky breath as *Little Drummer Boy* drifted through the air.

This had only happened one other time before, and good things didn't follow.

I used the counter to brace myself as his eyes stayed on mine.

His smile broke the spell as he studied me. "You're a

complicated soul, Daisy."

"Sorry. I just…"

Hunter shook his head. "Don't apologize. Just eat more taquitos."

I chuckled, lifting my beer. "And there's always this."

He nodded. "I do seem to make women I hang around do that more. Just ask my mom."

I laughed, shaking my head. "Hey, how is she? I haven't seen her around recently."

Hunter groaned, putting his forehead into his hands. "Don't get me started. They found the cruise life, and it's hard to find a two-week period where they're actually in town."

"I've heard that about cruising." I thought back to my mom. She'd always wanted to take a cruise. There were a lot of things she'd wanted to do, but then my world imploded. I took a bite of another ravioli. "I'd be up for camping in a trailer or RV. That would be fun. Don't get me wrong. Foxy is a great companion, but it can get cold in a tent by myself."

"You really go camping by yourself?"

I nodded. "Yeah. Sometimes, I can wrangle my cousin Jackson to go with me, but not so much now that he's married."

Hunter nodded. "You could always invite me."

I felt that charge run through us again, and I slowly

took another breath.

This wasn't the Hunter Knox I'd promised myself to walk away from.

This Hunter Knox undid every single cell in my body and made me think about a future different from what I had now.

And that scared me.

Chapter Six

Hunter

The electricity running between Daisy and me wasn't just intense. It was otherworldly, and I didn't understand it.

I knew I had a crush on her from last year, but every second I stayed with her, a frenzy of emotion stirred up that confused every rational thought I had.

Starting with… she lived in Buttercup Lake.

I lived in Madison, where I ran a business that needed me.

But we'd stopped decorating the tree long ago, talking nonstop while polishing off the snacks, and when I looked outside, I couldn't believe what I saw.

"Daisy, it's dark outside."

Her jaw dropped, and she giggled.

That sound would never get old.

"I can't believe you've been here for so long." She stood from the couch, and the pillow she'd been holding toppled to the carpet. "You need to get out more because I'm really not that interesting."

"And the tree isn't even finished," I added. "You know, I don't feel good leaving until we finish."

I stood from the couch, and as I bent over to pick up the pillow, she tripped over my arm.

Daisy gasped as she tumbled into my arms.

I dropped the pillow and pulled her upright to avoid her crashing into the tree.

Holding her in my arms made my entire body respond.

"I'm such a klutz," she muttered, looking into my eyes.

But I didn't let go.

"Daisy, you're so damn beautiful."

Her smile grew as she shook her head. "I think that third beer went straight to your head."

My arms looped around her waist as I looked into her eyes. Daisy's gaze dropped to my mouth.

Now was the time…

I had to kiss her.

Ding! Dong!

Her expression fell.

"Were you expecting someone?" I asked, letting her go.

She shook her head and shrugged. "Nope. Not a soul."

I walked over to the door with her as she opened it to see a small group of young kids with their parents standing behind them.

They immediately burst into caroling as Daisy knelt down to get a better view of the little ones belting out *Jingle Bells*.

She glanced at me over her shoulder as I rested my hand on her. There was something magical about the entire moment, and it really highlighted how much I missed the simple things. The hustle and bustle of the city had worn on me, but I think the relationship that left so many residual elements in my life weighed even heavier.

Everything about Daisy calmed me. She put her hand on mine and squeezed it softly as my fingers rested on her shoulder.

After the kids finished the last line of *Jingle Bells*, Daisy hopped up and started wildly clapping. I spotted a box of candy canes on a table, and Daisy followed my gaze with a nod. I tore open the box and held them out for the kids, who happily took one each.

We waved to their cold, brave parents as they all proceeded to the next house while Daisy softly closed the door.

"They were so cute," she nearly squealed.

I nodded, thinking about how amazing it would be to have kids one day. I always knew I wanted them, but wanting them was the easy part. Trying to find someone to have that journey with was completely different.

"I should probably head out. I've taken up enough of your day," I told her, even though I never wanted to leave.

"Did the kids give you hives?" she teased.

I shook my head, laughing. "Believe it or not, I love kids. I want a whole gaggle running around someday."

Her eyes locked on mine. "I never would have guessed."

I nodded. "What about you?"

"I've always hoped to have at least two someday, but I'd love three or four."

"I grew up in a busy house, and I miss it."

She nodded. "Me too."

"You have siblings?"

Sadness darted through her gaze, and she cleared her throat. "Um… no, but I…" Daisy's eyes met mine. "I had lots of cousins."

A strain tangled through the air between us, and I nodded. "Well, kids add a lot to any house."

She nodded, smiling. The sadness slid from her gaze as fast as it had come.

"Anyway, I'll be staying for dinner before you know it, so I should be on my way."

She laughed and shrugged. "I have nothing else to do for the next two weeks. I have no problem feeding you."

"Ah, that's right. How are you handling that?" I really didn't want to go back to my house because I honestly wasn't sure I'd see her again before I left.

"I filled out some paperwork to help supplement the income loss, but it won't do much." She shifted her weight and tugged on her sweater. "But I have a small savings that will get me through."

I nodded as ideas swirled in my head, and I tried to sound reasonable, not pushy.

"I know everyone loved working with you at my bar, and we could certainly use the help these next two weeks. It's always crazy right before the holidays."

She ran her fingers down her braid as she stared at the

floor. I couldn't gauge her reaction. Was she offended I offered, or did she feel like it was a handout? Because it certainly wasn't.

"I don't know if I could find a place short-term." Her eyes met with mine, and without thinking, my mouth opened.

"I have a spare bedroom. It's on the other side of my apartment, so you wouldn't even have to see me."

Daisy chuckled and shook her head, reaching for my cheek. She gave it a quick little pinch. "Why wouldn't I want to see this grinning mug every day?"

Every single thing about this woman drove me insane in the best possible way. I'd never felt like this around someone before, and here I just invited her to stay in my apartment for two weeks.

"Just sayin'," I joked. "I can be a little annoying."

Her eyes widened with a glint of fascination. "Me too. This is great. Maybe we can annoy the heck out of each other and get the Sunshine Breakfast Club off our backs."

I'd completely forgotten about them.

Oh, no. They would totally have a field day with this news.

"Maybe we don't mention that you're staying at my place."

She winked and pointed her index finger at me. "I see

where you're going with this. Totally agree, or they'll have us married off by Christmas."

Daisy slowly turned and looked around her house. "Are you sure about this?"

"Completely."

"And I do have to be back when the doors here open back up."

I nodded, loving how conscientious Daisy was. "Fully understand."

"You're not allergic to cats, right?"

"Not even a little." She pursed her lips into a thin line. "But I think it's best if I take my own car down there."

"Absolutely. I didn't want to ride in a car with you for a few hours, anyway."

She rolled her eyes and smiled. "You're missing out. I'm super good at packing road trip snacks."

"I'll have to remember that for when you invite me camping someday."

Daisy smiled and took a deep breath. "Are you sure you don't want to stay for dinner?"

I nodded. "Purrlock is probably wondering where her dinner is, so I should get going."

She smiled. "Ah, right. She won't be, you know, jealous of me... Will she?"

I chuckled and shook my head. "We'll find out."

Daisy wandered over to the kitchen and popped the last fried ravioli in her mouth. "You said you'd be leaving tomorrow or the following day?"

"Yeah. Maybe I'll head out tomorrow to get everything ready."

"You don't have to do that on account of me. Don't change your plans."

"I really didn't have many, but I'll head out tomorrow evening. I'll text my address to you so you have it."

She smiled. "This is really nice of you. Are you sure about this?"

"Completely sure."

"I'll have to tell Maya and Nina how wonderful their brother-in-law is."

"I think they know that." I flashed her a grin. "Which is why they're probably in cahoots with that book club to match us up."

Her hands whipped to her hips. "Oh, yeah? Then they must know that about me, too, since I'm your match."

The glint of mischief behind her gaze made me crazy for her. There was something so carefree about her. I wished I had even a sprinkle of that in my life.

Daisy closed her eyes and let out a groan. "I have a

confession."

"What's that?"

She blinked her eyes open and bit her lip, which was so darn sexy. Her gaze met mine, and the tiny curl to her lip was so cute.

But now that she was back to being my employee, I had to ignore those little traits that drove me crazy for her.

"I feel like karma is coming for me." She let out a slow, deep breath.

I cocked my head slightly. "How so?"

She squeezed her eyes shut and blurted out a sentence so fast I couldn't even decipher it.

"Try again." I walked toward her, closing the gap.

Daisy laughed and slowly tried again. "Behind the scenes, I was instrumental in setting up both of your brothers."

My eyes widened in surprise. "No way." I couldn't stop laughing. "Are you serious?"

She nodded, bringing her hands to her mouth. "I know how good the Sunshine Breakfast Club is at what they do."

"Does that worry you?"

She grinned. "Not too much."

"Okay, so we can beat them at their own game. When you get down to Madison, we'll set up completely platonic boundaries that we'll both follow."

She gave a strong nod. "Yes, we can avoid their trickery."

"Exactly. Who needs love?" I chuckled.

Daisy narrowed her eyes on me. "Love?"

"Or whatever they're trying to throw at us."

Daisy's wry smile widened. "Yeah, it's love."

"And at Christmas, of all times."

She chuckled. "The nerve."

"Okay, it's settled. We'll show them what we think of their Cupid and come out of the holidays unscathed, unloved, and ready for Valentine's Day."

Daisy clapped her hands and rubbed them together. "Sounds perfect."

I closed the gap between us and gave her a quick hug. "See you soon, buddy."

"See ya," Daisy said, smiling. "And thanks again for letting me work for you. It will help keep my savings intact."

I shook my head. "We're the lucky ones. You were amazing last year. I know everyone will be thrilled when they hear the good news. I'll text you later with my address." I started toward the door.

"Sounds good."

I could feel her gaze on me all the way to the door, and I wished that I could bottle up all these emotions and feelings washing over me. I was so worried that the moment I left her house, they'd disappear.

Daisy walked in front of me and opened the door, hanging on it as she smiled at me. "You know, Hunter? I think I was wrong about you."

"I hope I can make last year up to you, Daisy."

"You already have, Hunter." Her eyes stayed on mine, and if I hadn't just hired her again, I would have stopped to kiss her.

Chapter Seven

Daisy

After my battery had been changed out in Foxy, I'd packed everything I needed for the next two weeks, loaded it in my car, and took off for Madison this morning. I was only five minutes from Hunter's apartment, and my pulse quickened with each passing mile.

That day I'd spent with him decorating my tree, eating junk food, and drinking beer was something I didn't even know I needed. But for the first time in years, I didn't dread decorating the tree. Memories didn't overload me and turn me into a crying mess of epic proportions.

I'd made it through a tradition that, in recent years,

had been filled with pain and grief more than anything.

Sure, if you asked anybody who knew me if I ever had down days, they'd probably laugh as the word *never* tumbled from their lips.

But it wasn't true. One thing I'd come to understand in life was that often, the most outwardly happy and kind people carried the most heartache, shed the most hidden tears, and laughed the loudest. No one would ever expect that I'd run from any kind of love for nearly a decade or that I'd shied away from deep relationships.

Because I always laughed the loudest.

I also *always* volunteered to help the Sunshine Breakfast Club with their side gig of matchmaking so that I'd never be their target.

And look where that had gotten me.

I chuckled at the thought as my phone's GPS told me to turn at the next corner, where a modern, towering apartment building overlooked Lake Mendota. I pulled into the parking garage and looked for the parking spot number he'd given me.

My pulse started racing as each number ticked closer to the parking space. The moment I found it, I took a deep breath and slowly edged my way into the parking spot.

Staying with him would be fine. It was only two weeks.

Turning my car off, I let out the breath I'd been holding and loosened my fingers from the unintentional death grip on my steering wheel.

Hunter had sent me a code for the elevator and his apartment door. He'd mentioned he probably wouldn't be back from the bar in time to greet me, which took some of the stress out of things.

Not that I thought I'd walk into his apartment and suddenly want to kiss him.

Although, there were multiple occasions the other day when I'd hoped he'd pull me into his arms and kiss me.

It all goes back to that weird thing about Hunter.

He just looked like he was a kissable man.

I rolled my eyes at myself and silently vowed to behave.

I didn't do relationships, and I wasn't about to start now.

What I needed to do was get myself into his apartment, unpack, and read the chapters Millie told me about when she handed me the book. The one thing I knew I needed to do was stay in the loop with this club. I had to stay on top of things, one step ahead of them, or they'd use it to their advantage.

I climbed out of my car and opened the trunk to see

my two suitcases and a backpack. I glanced at the elevator across from where I'd parked and debated whether I could make it.

Yeah, I could balance them all.

As I delicately placed the second bag on the first one and looped my arms through the backpack, I heard a man humming a Christmas carol a few cars down.

"Hey, there," he said, giving a wave. "Need any help with those?"

I scowled. "No. I'm fine. Thanks."

"You sure? I don't mind." His smile widened, and I remembered all those stories about serial killers with good smiles.

"Totally fine, but thanks." I rolled my bags toward the elevator with Mr. Good Deeds behind me.

As I struggled with the door, he quickly dashed in front of me and opened the door.

"Here, I've got that for you." He grinned as I slid by him with my bags.

"Thanks."

"Floor?" he asked, standing next to me.

I knew better than to tell strangers where I lived, but he was about to get on the elevator with me. I didn't need to be weirder than I already had been. Plus, there were plenty of cameras.

"P."

He whistled. "Big time."

I tilted my head in confusion. "How so?"

"The penthouse."

"Oh, right. I didn't even put two and two together. P, penthouse. Gotcha."

The elevator dinged, and I rolled right into the carriage.

"So, are you friends with Hunter?" he asked.

"Yeah. Something like that."

He nodded as I pushed in my code to ride up to P.

"He's certainly not around much now that he's not with that woman with dark hair."

I chuckled. "You mean Brielle?"

He snapped his fingers. "That's her name."

"Are you friends with Hunter?" I asked.

"I try to hit up his bar a couple of times a month. Good drinks. Good food. Good company. If that makes us friends, then yes. My name is Dave."

"Good to meet you, Dave."

I wasn't going to give him my name, and thankfully, the elevator opened on his floor just in time.

"Have a nice evening," I told him as he walked off

with a wave.

The doors closed slowly with a smack and carried me up to P.

I chuckled, realizing I didn't even know his place was on the top floor.

He certainly didn't mention it, but what would he say? It kind of goes with the whole flashy living thing, I guessed.

As the doors opened, I saw an apartment door at the end of the hall to the right and one to the left. I looked down at my phone and determined that Hunter's penthouse was to the right. I rolled my suitcases down the spacious hallway and stopped in front of his door.

I stared at my phone again and typed in the code for the door. It clicked, and I pushed it open to see an expansive hallway leading into the living area. Floor-to-ceiling windows encased the entire two-story room, which showcased a beautiful view of the lake. Hardwood floors stretched as far as the eye could see.

This was spectacular. He'd said it was modern and cold, but the natural light warmed things right up for me.

As I slowly rolled my suitcases into the room, I turned to see a large kitchen with grey cabinets, white counters, and stainless-steel appliances. Above that was a loft overlooking the living area with a dark metal, sleek railing.

I looked around to see a staircase with a matching railing leading up the stairs. I rolled my bags over and took the first one off to haul up the stairs.

But first, I turned around to appreciate the expansive view of the lake.

"This is so beautiful," I whispered, noticing a few photographs on the wall before a yowl scared me to death.

I turned around and looked up the stairs to see Purrlock staring down at me as if I were a burglar.

"It's okay, Purrlock. Your daddy is letting me stay here."

She sat and curled her tail around her as if to challenge me to a duel. I had visions of getting up the stairs and her wrapping her legs around my ankle, refusing to let go.

"I'm coming up, Purrlock. You just lead the way," I said calmly, taking each step carefully until I made it to the regal white cat.

Meow. She tilted her head, and I realized she had one hazel eye and one blue eye.

"Ah, you're so pretty, aren't you?"

Purrlock stood and arched her back as she brushed up against my suitcase. "Okay, lead the way to the guestroom."

Surprisingly, Purrlock led the way, but not before I stopped to take in the view. A bonus room at the top of the stairs had a sectional and a glass coffee table. I might sneak there tonight to start the book.

Purrlock meowed at the opening to a bedroom, and I smiled.

"Good girl, Purrlock." I rolled my suitcase right into the guest room and froze.

A constant stream of water pattering onto tile echoed from a door slightly propped along the far wall, and then Hunter's voice echoed into the room as he sang *All I Want for Christmas is You*.

The water turned off, but he kept singing as I glared at the cat and pointed. "You did this," I hissed.

Purrlock hopped onto the bed and stretched her sleek body as Hunter's singing turned to a whistle, and I started to spin around.

But not before Hunter walked into his bedroom.

I shrieked, and Hunter jumped, gripping a white towel around his waist.

"You're here," I squealed, hopping in place and closing my eyes.

"Yeah, I got home early. Surprise." Hunter laughed. "You know, you can open your eyes. I'm completely covered."

"No, you're not. You have abs of steel and a chest

someone could play ping-pong on." I shielded my eyes and searched for my suitcase to roll out of the room. "I shouldn't be looking at my half-naked boss before my shift tomorrow."

But. Oh. My. Word. He looked sensational.

Hunter's laughter rumbled through the air. "You could look at it as if your boss is half-dressed, you know."

I chuckled, bringing my eyes to his. "Do you spend all your time in the gym or something?"

He reached for a sweater from the bed and pulled it over his head. "No, but when I'm stressed, I go there for an hour or so."

"Are you stressed a lot?"

Hunter's grin widened as he ran his fingers through his wet hair. "A few times a week."

I stood frozen, staring at my extremely sexy boss who had a towel wrapped around his waist and a wool sweater on top.

He looked ridiculous.

And sexy.

My cheeks warmed as I stood staring, but my legs seriously stopped working.

"Okay, I'm obviously in the wrong room." I cleared my throat and reached for the handle of my suitcase to roll away. "So, I won't be following Purrlock around the apartment anymore."

Hunter chuckled. "You're blaming the cat?"

"I don't know if I'm going to be able to look you in your eyes again," I joked.

"Good thing I had the towel wrapped around my waist."

I smiled. "I have a good imagination. That's the problem, not the towel."

Hunter laughed and shook his head. "Off to a good start. Your room is across the hall."

I ramped down the embarrassment and scowled at Purrlock. "You know, she's the culprit."

Hunter's brows rose. "You're seriously going to blame Purrlock Holmes?"

I adjusted my backpack and pulled the suitcase out the door. To my surprise, Purrlock followed me across the hall to the real guest room.

The room was really pretty, with a bright white duvet, powder blue pillows, and a matching throw draped over the end of the bed. I pushed my suitcase into the empty closet and shrugged off my backpack as Purrlock jumped onto the bed.

"If you were truly my buddy, Purrlock, you would have clawed that towel right off him," I teased, scratching the cat's chin. She responded with purrs, and I smiled.

"What was that?" Hunter asked. "You need some towels?"

I spun around and crossed both arms over my chest.

"Were you eavesdropping?"

Hunter glanced at his cat. "Not intentionally. I didn't know you were having a private conversation with her, but I'll keep that in mind when I'm roaming my halls."

I chuckled. "Please do."

"But I actually came over to ask if you've eaten dinner. I brought some chicken wings home."

"Chicken wings?" My stomach growled. "That's like my favorite food."

"Spicy?"

I nodded. "Even better."

"I'll throw them in the air fryer, and they should crisp right up."

"Well, thank you. That's really nice of you, and I promise you won't have to buy me dinner when I'm here."

"It's my pleasure." He glanced around the room. "Is there anything else you need? Towels are in the linen closet across from the bathroom at the end of the hall."

"I'm set. Thanks." I glanced at the white cat. "I just have one more bag to grab from downstairs."

"Oh, I can get that for you."

"Thanks." I sat on the bed next to Purrlock. "I met your neighbor."

"Evelyn? She's down the hall and such a sweetheart."

"No. Dave." I shrugged. "He was quite friendly, but I didn't trust him. He gave me the creeps."

Hunter laughed and shook his head. "Then you have good taste. Brielle slept with him."

My jaw dropped. "No way."

"Yup."

I shivered at the thought. "I'm so sorry. You weren't kidding when you said she wasn't faithful."

Hunter's eyes stayed on mine as if he were trying to figure me out, but I was pretty transparent. Or I thought I was.

"Everyone at the bar is ecstatic you're helping out for a couple of weeks."

"I'm excited to see everyone again."

He tapped the doorframe. "Okay. I'll be right back with your bag."

"Thanks. My book is in that one, and I have strict orders to read eight chapters."

He chuckled as his phone rang. He pulled it out of his pocket and started down the hall. It sounded like his mom was on the other end of the phone, and his voice quieted.

My stomach knotted at the simplicity of it all.

Something I took for granted.

A call from my mom.

I ran my hands over Purrlock's silky fur and willed myself not to cry.

Chapter Eight

Hunter

Things certainly stay lively with Daisy around the apartment. I heard her humming *Silent Night* in the loft bonus area, and it brought a smile to my lips.

I'd always felt like this apartment was cold, but I noticed since Daisy had arrived how much warmer things felt.

Surprisingly, Purrlock hadn't left her side, which was a relief because all she ever did to anyone else was hiss at them. I just hadn't wanted to tell Daisy that before she arrived.

As I flipped the chicken wings, I thought about my mom's call. She and Dad rarely came to town, but I was glad they were making the trek down. I still wasn't sure why, though. It sounded like they had *The Nutcracker* tickets or wanted to get some, and then my Dad suggested a hotel and made a weekend of it.

I wasn't really sure, but it sounded like they'd be arriving on Friday night.

When the humming stopped, I turned around and looked out the window, where I could see Daisy's reflection upstairs. She'd curled up with a book in one of my favorite places in the apartment.

I grabbed some silverware and set the table, trying not to overthink things. But from the moment Daisy walked in on me, I couldn't help but wonder what else might happen while she stayed here.

I put the plates out just as my phone rang. Pulling it out of my pocket, I cringed when I saw the name pop up.

Brielle

It was like she had a sixth sense for these types of things. I let it go to voicemail, but she called again. I ignored that call, too, and bent over to look at the chicken wings in the fryer.

I hadn't heard from her in over a year. I had no desire to hear from her ever again, and last I'd heard, she'd found a guy who happened to be a hedge fund manager in New York.

The air fryer dinged, and I opened the fridge and

pulled out a salad I'd made.

"Hey, Daisy. Dinner is ready."

"I'll be right down." Her voice rang through the apartment and completely wiped away the bad taste I had from Brielle's calls.

I put the chicken wings and salad on the table and glanced toward the stairs.

Daisy bounded down the steps with Purrlock in her arms, and I was shocked.

She set the cat down and smiled. "What? Why are you looking at me like that?"

"Purrlock doesn't like people."

Daisy chuckled. "Then what does that make me?"

Her eyes landed on the table, and she grinned. "Now that is what I'm talking about. How many wings did you make?"

"I think thirty."

She snickered. "And I could probably eat them all."

"Just so you know, I ate every piece of fudge you gave me."

"Really? In two days? I'm impressed. That was a full batch."

I chuckled, nodding my head. "Keep feeding me like that, and what you saw earlier will vanish."

"I'll have to keep that in mind. You know, in a completely platonic way."

"Right. Exactly."

She took a seat as I poured some water into her glass.

"Did you want a beer or anything?"

She nodded. "Hey, how did that gingerbread beer from your brother work out?"

I grabbed two bottles out of the fridge and set them down on the table.

"Not well." I laughed. "It was the worst beer I've ever had in my life."

She gasped. "You didn't tell him that, did you?"

"No. I softened it."

I wanted to tell her I worked on my delivery method after she'd mentioned I was too direct, but I kept that to myself and took a sip of beer as she dug into the chicken wings.

She took a bite of chicken. "Mmm. So good. These are from the bar."

"Yeah. I tend to order them from the bar more times than I care to admit."

"They are addicting." She nodded. "So, I'm getting a pretty clear picture of who Hunter is. You spend your days at the gym, working off stress, and then you come home and gorge on chicken wings. You've got it made."

"I don't know, but that smorgasbord of snacks the other day was pretty tasty." I eyed her and couldn't help but love what I saw. Daisy put joy into the world. No doubt about it.

She held the tiny wing in both hands and smiled. "You are a lot less fancy than I would have guessed. I mean, apart from the penthouse apartment, glitzy SUV, and..." She stopped herself and shrugged. "You're just full of surprises."

"I could say the same."

"Nah. I'm as boring as they come. Give me a good book, and I'm the happiest you'll ever see me."

"Do you stick to the Sunshine Breakfast Club's choices?" I took a bite of chicken.

Daisy shook her head. "No. I veer off course a lot. Before the one Millie insisted on me reading, I had started a thriller."

I nodded. "I love a good thriller."

Her eyes grew huge. "You read?"

"It surprises you that I'm literate?"

She chuckled. "You just didn't strike me as a guy who cracks a spine very often."

"I guess we have a lot to learn about each other," I said softly, noticing some hot sauce on her chin.

I reached over with a napkin and dabbed it off for her.

"You had a little something-something."

"Aw, thanks. There's those manners again."

"You just bring it out in me."

Purrlock let out a huge meow, and I rolled my eyes. "Parenthood calls."

I stood and walked over to my cat's food dish and filled it up while my cell phone rang on the table.

Daisy glanced at the flashing screen, and her expression fell. Instantly, I knew who blinked on my cell.

She reached for her bottle of beer and took a swig as I set down Purrlock's food and tried not to panic.

I made my way over to the table and grabbed my phone. "You saw?"

Daisy nodded slowly and lifted her shoulders. "But it's none of my business."

I waited for Daisy to bring her gaze to mine, but she didn't.

"It kind of is your business, and I don't know why she's calling. I haven't heard from her in over a year."

Daisy nodded and grabbed another wing. "Like I said, it's none of my business."

My phone buzzed.

"Ope. Sounds like she left a message." Daisy flashed a wry smile. "You can go ahead and call her back. I can hide out in my room."

"Daisy, I don't want to talk to her. There's nothing left to say."

"But you could if you wanted to. That's all I'm saying."

"I know, and I don't want to."

Daisy nodded her head and smiled. "Okay. I totally believe you."

"My mom and dad are coming down to Madison this weekend." I tried to change the subject to something neutral.

"That's cool." Her eyes landed on me, and she grinned. "I'll hide out in the guest room until my shift."

I chuckled. "You don't have to do that."

"You know she's part of the club, don't you?" She looked like she wanted to say something else.

"The book club? Yeah, I know. But it's my mom. I trust her not to throw any shenanigans our way."

She slipped her leg underneath her and took a swig of beer. "Sounds like a reconnaissance mission, if you ask me."

I laughed. "Seriously? There'd be nothing to report."

"Never say never. You'd be amazed at what can be gleaned from a simple run-in. So, an entire weekend trip sounds very suspicious. You could let your gaze linger on me too long at the bar, and your mom could report you have a crush when you really just wanted to see what drink I was pouring."

I chuckled, shaking my head.

"You do know who put forth the idea of finding partners for Cash and Beckett, right?" She smirked and leaned back in her chair, glancing around the dining area. "She might be interested to know that you're in touch with Brielle, though."

Ah-ha! Daisy did care.

I shrugged, grinning. "I'm not in touch with her."

"Your phone says otherwise. Not that it's my business."

I laughed harder, shaking my head. The tension between us was palpable.

"But I bet your mom would be thrilled to know either way." She winked at me.

My brows raised. "But she won't know because there is nothing to share."

Daisy laughed with a mischievous glint in her eyes. "We shall see."

"You wouldn't tell her." It was more of a question than a statement.

Daisy laughed her answer.

And the chemistry between us only heightened. It was

like some crazy cat-and-mouse game of wills.

"You don't owe me anything, especially not an explanation. If anything, I owe you. You've given me rides when Foxy broke down. You helped me decorate my tree. You made me feel better about temporarily losing my job. And you gave me a new one." She patted my hand. "So, your secret is safe with me. I won't tell your mom you're talking to your ex again."

I groaned and couldn't help but laugh.

"Isn't there some old ex that I can dig up and taunt you with?" I teased.

She took another bite of a wing and shook her head. "No, I'm smarter than that."

"Which part?"

Daisy's eyes connected with mine, and I felt that familiar electricity bolting through me. "I told you. I don't do relationships."

I nodded. "You've mentioned it, but I don't know if I believe it."

She flashed a sly grin. "You can even ask my cousin... or shoot, ask Great Uncle Carter. He knows. I mean, I spent most of my days and nights taking care of him. He has the inside scoop."

"I'll have to remember that next time I'm in Buttercup

Lake."

"Good." Daisy gave a quick nod and looked out the window toward Lake Mendota. "I would have told you earlier, except you had me all distracted with your towel strewn carelessly over your body, but your apartment is absolutely beautiful. I don't find it cold at all."

I smiled. "That's because you're here."

"What's that supposed to mean?"

I shrugged. "I don't know how to explain it, but you just light up every place you're in. You make things feel better than they actually are."

She sat back in the chair and looked at me. "That's one of the sweetest things anyone has ever said to me."

"It's true." I clasped my hands together. "But I hope one day, you'll tell me why you're not into relationships."

She relaxed a little and nodded. "Maybe there will come a time."

I reached for her hand, and it wasn't even meant to be romantic, but as she kept her fingers laced with mine, I wondered what she wasn't telling me.

"I want to be that guy you can trust. The guy you can tell anything to." I studied Daisy, unsure of what I was looking for. "And if that means keeping me in the friend zone, I'll do it because something with you is better than nothing."

She nodded, keeping her hand in mine. "It's been easy so far. I like this friendship. I just hope tomorrow doesn't ruin it."

"Why would it?" I drew my hand back from hers and smiled.

"Because when you were my boss last year, you weren't exactly a peach."

The words stung, no matter how true they were. "Have I made up for that yet?"

"With these chicken wings? Yes, but don't blow it."

Chapter Nine

Daisy

The moment I arrived at the bar, everyone was so friendly, and I was super shocked they remembered me. A sparkling silver Christmas tree took up the back corner, and silver ornaments hanging from the ceiling tastefully added to the Christmas spirit.

Perry, who was the lead bartender, hugged me and gave me an apron that read *Knox Bar and Grill*.

"Oh, these are new," I said, dangling the black apron in front of me. "I like it."

Perry smiled as a large group of people entered the bar.

I was instantly back in the groove, taking orders, chatting with the locals, and making drinks as fast as I could.

The new bar manager, Michelle, introduced herself in between customers, and she seemed super friendly and competent. I understood why Hunter felt like he could actually leave Madison now and again.

As I shook my tenth peppermint martini, Hunter's laugh rumbled through me, and I almost dropped the shaker. His eyes connected with mine, and he flashed a huge grin.

Okay, so far, so good.

Maybe he wasn't bound to repeat his grumpiness from last year.

I watched Hunter make the rounds through the bar, visiting with patrons, cracking jokes, and spending time in the kitchen. It was such a stark difference from last year, but I didn't want to get my hopes up.

The night flew by. Around midnight, the last customer left, and Michelle looked at Perry and then at me. "You did phenomenally well for your first night. Are you sure we can't steal you away from Buttercup Lake?"

I chuckled, untying the apron. "I think my great uncle and cousin would miss me fiercely."

"I understand. It's really beautiful up there too."

I nodded, wondering where Hunter had wandered off

to.

"I'll take care of the cleanup," I told them. "It will give me time to unwind."

Perry frowned. "Are you sure?"

"Totally." I nodded as Michelle looked at me for approval. "I'm serious. My mind is racing from tonight, and I just need time to mindlessly mop the floor."

"Have fun with that," Perry said, laughing as he untied his apron. "I'll see you on Saturday. I have tomorrow off." Perry untied his apron and gave a quick wave goodbye as Michelle wiped down the bar. "Usually, we have three bartenders on duty, but Carly called in sick tonight. You should have two bartenders on the floor tomorrow, and I can always step in if things get hectic. I have you scheduled for Sunday off."

"Oh, I can work on Sunday," I offered.

Michelle smiled and shook her head. "Hunter specifically said it was a day off for you."

"Okay. Well, the boss has spoken."

Michelle chuckled, holding the rag. "Yes, he has. On that note, I think I'm going to scramble home and hug my pug for the rest of the night."

I smiled, walking toward the storage closet to grab the broom. "Sounds like perfection."

"Hunter's still around if you need him. Last I saw, he was in the office."

"Okay. Thanks again. It was wonderful meeting you."

Michelle nodded and wandered through the kitchen to the back door while I took out all the supplies. I filled the bucket with soap and water for when it was time for me to mop, smelling the strong scent of pine.

I walked over to the stereo and found a Christmas station as I started sweeping the bar area first. It wasn't long before I was dancing with my broom, belting out some Bing Crosby, when I nearly bumped into Hunter.

My cheeks blushed, and I looked into his brilliant blue eyes. "How long have you been standing there?"

"Long enough to have had my night made."

I chuckled, rolling my eyes. "I'm starting to get the distinct feeling that you just like watching me embarrass myself."

Hunter chuckled, and that low rumble of a laugh he had tickled all parts of me, which made me look away.

I didn't want him to think that I had a crush on him.

Or that I couldn't stop wondering what it would be like to kiss him.

"You finish sweeping that side," —he pointed at the large seating area— "and I'll start mopping over here so we can go home sooner."

My brows knitted together as I leaned against my broom. "You don't have to stay. I volunteered to do this. It's my therapy."

"You don't strike me as someone who needs therapy."

"Ha, little do you know." I winked at him and felt my insides turn into a sloppy mess of emotions. This was where most people could probably confess their innermost secrets and feel much better about themselves and life.

But I wasn't one of those.

"Did seeing me naked in the towel mess with you that much?" he teased.

"You wish." I chuckled, lifting all the chairs onto the tables.

"Maybe I do."

"You're impossible."

Hunter squeezed the mop and followed my steps as I started sweeping.

Before I knew it, we'd covered the entire bar, and he was already rolling the bucket away to dump it out.

We made a good team.

I shoved everything back into the supply closet as he rolled the empty bucket toward me.

"Now, how about dinner?" he asked, his eyes resting on mine.

"It's after midnight."

Hunter grinned and nodded. "Close to one o'clock now."

I looked around the sparkling clean bar. "Well, I *am* kind of hungry."

"Awesome. I had the chef whip up our cobb salad for each of us and some of our famous garlic bread."

"Maybe a leopard can change its spots after all," I teased.

He laughed, walking toward the kitchen and disappearing before returning with a plate in each hand, making his way to the counter, where I'd pulled down two stools.

"This was thoughtful of you," I told Hunter as he sat next to me.

"I want to hear all about your first day. Michelle said you were incredible."

I lifted my shoulders. "What can I say? I remember instructions well."

Bemusement filled Hunter's gaze. "That's right. You have a memory as good as an elephant's, possibly a dolphin's."

I laughed, shaking my head as I took a bite of salad. "So, you do listen to what I say."

His gaze caught mine, and I suddenly wanted to tell him everything about my life. I wanted to open up to him like I'd never done before, but I couldn't.

The logical side of me knew I was only here for two more weeks.

Friends or not, I didn't need to unload my entire life's history on this poor, unsuspecting guy.

"So, my parents want to have dinner tomorrow at my place," he started.

"That should work out perfectly since I'm here tomorrow."

Hunter smiled, nodding. "True."

"And Saturday, they're attending *The Nutcracker.*"

"Perfect." I took a bite of bacon and enjoyed the smokiness. "Oh, that reminds me. Michelle said I couldn't work on Sunday. Is there a reason?"

Hunter grinned and leaned closer. "I was hoping you'd attend the Christmas tree lighting with me. It's kind of a big deal."

"I mean, sure. I can do that."

"Awesome."

"Is there something more I should know about this

ceremony or…?"

Hunter's smile grew. "No. It's just down the street at the Waterfront Park."

"Okay, I'll dress warm."

"My parents will be there."

I couldn't hide my surprise. "Are you sure that's a smart idea?"

Hunter shook his head and took a bite of salad. "No, not at all. But they want to be there."

"This must be some tree lighting."

He nodded with a mischievous smile. "It kind of is."

I focused on my salad and tried to push away the feelings floating over me. The pull to him was hard to ignore, but I didn't understand the root of it all.

Was it the holidays?

The kissable lips?

The Sunshine Breakfast Club?

I blew out a gust of air, and he chuckled. "A lot on your mind?"

"You could say that."

"Anything you want to share with me?" he asked, turning on the stool and pushing his salad plate away.

"You know how you're tired of being alone?" I asked softly.

He nodded, letting out a sigh. "Indeed, I do."

"I think I have a similar problem."

Hunter's brows furrowed, which only made him look sexier. "I thought you didn't do relationships."

"I don't, but I hate being alone. I think that's why I joined the Sunshine Breakfast Club, helped out my great-uncle, volunteered at the animal rescue, and worked extra shifts. The only time I like being by myself is when I have a good book, and that's only because even then, I'm not alone."

My words hung in the air as the Christmas music lingered around us.

Hunter reached for my hand and linked his fingers with mine. The sensations rolling through me warmed my body as I brought my gaze to his.

"Why do you think that is, Daisy?"

I let out a slow breath. "Because I like being happy. I pride myself on being the cheery one."

"You are that in every sense of the word." He nodded in agreement.

"But when I'm by myself, I'm not happy at all. In fact, I'm sad."

Concern spread through Hunter's gaze as he pulled my hand to his lap. He didn't say a word. He waited for me to continue.

I drew a deep breath and nodded as the uncertainty vanished. "When you came over to help me decorate the tree, it was the biggest relief."

"Really?"

I nodded. "It's usually a sad time for me, and I thought it was always going to be like that. I mean, it has been for years."

"I had no idea, Daisy. I'm so sorry."

"Don't be. Having you there this last time gave me hope."

Hunter's gaze stayed on mine, and it felt like the weight of the world was lifting. "How did I do that?"

"You showed me that new memories can coexist."

"Daisy, what happened to make the holidays so sad?"

I pursed my lips and felt tears balancing on the brim of my lids as I tried to blink them away.

"My mom and brother were taken away from me in a car accident." Saying the words aloud didn't release the flood of tears I'd expected.

My eyes met Hunter's as he studied me closely, giving me my space. "We were decorating the tree, and we ran out of candy canes. They went to buy some more and never came home."

I toyed with the napkin on the counter and let the

words rattle around.

"I had absolutely no idea, Daisy. None whatsoever. I'm stunned."

I drew a deep breath and let it out. "I haven't told a soul that in years. I just… It doesn't fit who I want to be."

Hunter frowned, cocking his head slightly. "What do you mean?"

"I don't want to be the person swallowed up by grief. I want to be the exact opposite." I smiled at Hunter. "And for the most part, I am."

"Unless you're by yourself," he said softly.

"Exactly." I looked around the bar. "So, these two weeks are a gift because sitting home without a job would have been torture."

"Daisy, you're extraordinary. I've always sensed it, but I didn't know why."

"I don't feel very less than ordinary most days," I whispered. "But I'm working on it."

"You have every right to feel how you want to feel," Hunter said, keeping his eyes steady on mine. "But I hope I can show you that your loss didn't define you."

A ripple of sadness swept over me as I thought about my brother and mom. "We'd always been the three musketeers. My dad took off when we were young, and my mom did everything in her power to make our lives amazing. And they were." I smiled at Hunter. "We didn't have a lot of money, but we didn't need it. Not with a mom like ours."

Hunter reached over and wiped away the tears that I didn't even realize had spilled down my cheeks.

Chapter Ten

Hunter

I wanted to take away all the pain and hurt that threatened to swallow Daisy up, but I knew I couldn't.

I could only provide hope that things would get better.

One day.

Things would be a new normal.

We'd gone back to my place last night, and I woke up to the smell of bacon permeating the apartment. Purrlock was nowhere to be seen, and I had a hunch she was Daisy's new sidekick.

After I brushed my teeth and showered, I made my

way down the stairs to see Daisy in the kitchen, holding a red bowl in one hand and mixing with the other.

"Hello, handsome… in a completely platonic way," she teased, setting the bowl down. "Hope you like pancakes."

"Who wouldn't love them?" I came up behind her just as she stepped back. Daisy's body pressed against mine, and I smelled the sweet scent all her own. Somedays, there was a hint of rose, and other days, like today, vanilla. "You smell good."

She laughed, but I noticed she didn't inch away. "I spilled vanilla on my jammies, so…"

"And here I thought you just smelled good."

Daisy spun around, her gaze catching mine as she bit her bottom lip briefly. "I wanted to say thank you for last night."

I jolted in surprise. "You don't have to thank me for being a friend, Daisy. It meant a lot to me that you opened up."

She set the bowl down and smiled. "Really?"

"Of course."

She turned on the stove and put a skillet on the burner. "Well, I'm not used to it, so… sorry if it turned things weird."

"On the contrary."

I leaned against the counter and watched her scoop

the batter from the bowl before pouring it into the hot pan.

"You know, you could really do with some Christmas decorations around here."

I looked around the bare apartment and smiled. "You think?"

"Yeah, even I faked it."

"Fake it till you make it."

Daisy chuckled. "Always been my motto. Now, watch this."

She took the skillet and waved it back and forth before flipping the pancake in the air and catching it back in the skillet. I snapped a photo of her instantly and couldn't believe what I'd caught in action. Daisy looked adorable in the shot.

Daisy grinned at me. "Impressed?"

"Extremely." I laughed. "And now I get to keep it forever."

Daisy chuckled. "My brother taught me that. He figured out how to do it when he was like thirteen. Whenever I tried to do his infamous flip, the batter would explode everywhere. But then I made it my mission."

I smiled, knowing that this was Daisy's way of slowly opening up to me, and I felt extremely privileged.

She slid the first pancake onto a plate, opened the oven, placed three pieces of bacon next to the pancake, and handed me the plate.

"Syrup and butter are on the table."

"Thanks." I took a seat, watching Daisy make another pancake.

"Anyway, my brother became the man of the house as soon as he figured out that we didn't have one," she continued. "So, you can imagine what it was like having a seven-year-old barking orders, changing lightbulbs, and telling me to clean up my toys."

"Was he older or younger?"

"Ethan was one year older than me." She smiled, brushing some hair back from her face as she took the skillet and flipped the pancake. "We were both home from college when the accident happened. My mom was so happy to have us both home for the holidays."

An ache grew in my chest. "I bet."

A smile touched her lips as she slid her pancake onto a plate and plopped some bacon next to it. She walked over and sat across from me as I spread butter on my pancake.

I took a bite, and the pancake melted in my mouth. "So good, Daisy."

She grinned and poured syrup onto her pancake right when my phone rang.

I froze, remembering I never dealt with Brielle's

message and hoped it wasn't her again.

Relief flooded through me when I saw my sister's name pop up on the screen.

"It's Evie, my sister," I told Daisy as I answered the cell on speaker.

"*Who are you talking to so early in the morning?*" my sister teased.

"Just a friend who's staying here for a week. Why?"

"*It sounded like a she.*" Evie chuckled. "*And you don't ever have a* she *over when I call.*"

My hands fumbled for the phone to take my sister off speaker, but Daisy's brows rose. With everything she'd shared with me this morning, the least I could do was let myself get roasted by my sister.

"She's filling in at the bar," I explained.

"*And staying at your house? Mom and Dad ought to get a rise out of this one when they show up tonight.*"

Daisy beamed at me, completely amused.

"*Anyway, I'm calling because I got a message from Brielle.*"

I groaned into the phone, and Evie laughed. "*I felt the same way, but she said she really needed to talk with you and that she'd left you a message already.*"

"Yeah." I glanced at Daisy, who craned her neck

forward. "But that's how she always worked her way back in, so I just ignored the call."

Evie sighed into the phone. "*You know I'm not Team Brielle by any means, but her voice sounded... strained, different.*"

I hadn't even listened to the message. "Okay. I'll deal with it."

"*As long as I don't have to talk to her,*" Evie nearly sang into the phone. "*And by the way, is it Daisy at your house?*"

I shook my head. "Unbelievable."

"*Tell her hi.*"

"Hi, Evie," Daisy chimed in.

"*I hope to see you when I'm in town at Christmas,*" Evie told Daisy as if I no longer existed.

"That would be great. I'm only in Madison for two weeks until everything's fixed at Styx."

"*Yeah. I heard about that. I'm so glad everyone made it out okay.*"

Of course, she'd heard about it.

"You knew Daisy was here the whole time?" I asked my sister.

"*You actually had to ask me that? Do you really think Mom and Dad were dying to drive two hours to watch The*

Nutcracker when the community center puts on their own every year?"

"How do they know?" I chuckled, shaking my head. "And why do they think they need to be here?"

"Didn't you say you had something special happening on Sunday?" Evie continued. *"Maybe they figured if you want Daisy there, then she must be special. Ergo, they ought to be involved, too."*

Daisy couldn't keep the grin off her face as I slumped in the chair.

"There are no secrets in Buttercup Lake," I muttered, and my sister giggled.

"And I don't even live there," Evie added.

"For the record, Evie. Daisy and I are strictly friends. Platonic."

"Lots of boundaries," Daisy added over the phone.

Evie chuckled. *"Whatever the kids are calling it nowadays. Just make sure to take care of the Brielle call. I don't want to be afraid it's her every time the phone rings."*

"I know the feeling, but I'll get it figured out." Just the thought of having to call her made me grumpy. This had been how she'd always wormed her way back into a relationship with me.

But I was done.

"*Love ya, Hunt.*"

And just like that, Evie hung up the phone while Daisy stared at me in disbelief.

Daisy chuckled, holding onto the table. "I feel like I just experienced a Category Three hurricane."

"Evie has that effect on people."

Daisy circled her finger on the table. "So, it must be important if Brielle keeps calling."

"I don't know what could be earth-shattering after not speaking for over a year." I drew a breath. "Unless she got dumped."

Daisy grimaced. "Sorry about that. Don't hold back on account of me."

My eyes connected with Daisy's. Vulnerability dripped from her, and it made every part of my body want to shield her from any more hurt in this world, but I knew that wasn't how the world worked.

"Daisy, I know this is a new friendship between us, but I haven't felt this... connected. Ever." I shook my head. "The only thing I'm holding back is how I feel for you."

Surprise washed over her features as a blush crept up her neck. "I wasn't expecting that."

"It's the truth, and I can't keep pretending. You should know." I let out a deep breath and looked out at the lake. "But I'd rather keep a friendship with you forever than have you jump into something you're not certain about."

She nodded slowly, but her gaze never left mine.

It felt like the entire world drifted away, only leaving the tension of my confession lingering in the air.

But it didn't matter.

"My point is that I care about you, Daisy."

Her beautiful smile surfaced again. "I care about you too, Hunter."

"And the reason I was a jerk last year was because I had a huge crush on you all the while my ex was hanging around the bar. Your laughter made my days better. Your joy filled my normally dead heart."

She chuckled, keeping her gaze on me.

"And I just didn't know what to do because you're Daisy. The woman everyone in town loves, and I'm Hunter. The guy who can't maintain a stable relationship to save my life." I shook my head. "I wish I hadn't let a year go by, but here we are."

Daisy's brows knitted together. "You had a crush on me, so you were mean to me?"

"Yes, I know. Very fifth grade of me." I shook my head. "But in my defense, I also knew Brielle could make a scene, and you didn't need that hassle."

Daisy's mouth lifted into a lopsided grin. "I can handle that explanation."

I couldn't hide my surprise. "You can?"

"And I appreciate not having drama. I've had enough of that to last a lifetime." She turned her gaze to the window and walked over to look at the view.

After a few minutes, she turned slowly and looked at me. "Well, ever since I stepped foot into your bar last year, I've dreamed of what it would be like to kiss you."

My heart quickened, and it felt like all the air in the room had been sucked out. I attempted a deep breath, but all I could think about were Daisy's words.

"Even after I was a Scrooge?"

She chuckled, hugging herself as the chill from the window came through. "Probably more so because I knew it would be completely unattainable at that point."

"Wow."

"I'm big on personality, and I wasn't sure I liked yours, but I still couldn't stop thinking about those lips of yours."

Her words were driving me wild.

"And when I saw you at the community center earlier this week, your darn lips were front and center again."

"But I hadn't redeemed myself yet."

She smiled. "Nope. You hadn't."

I slowly made my way over to Daisy. With each step closer, my body longed for something it shouldn't.

Daisy looked up into my eyes, and I put my hands on each of her shoulders. "We come from very different worlds. You like penthouses. I like small houses."

"You like provocative names for vehicles, while I like complicated pet names."

She chuckled. "I pretend like you're not obnoxiously good-looking."

"While I pretend that my heart doesn't stop every time that I see you."

She rested her hands on my chest, keeping her gaze on mine. "What does this mean?"

I smiled and shook my head. "I don't know, but we can't let the Sunshine Breakfast Club get wind of this, or they'll take complete credit."

Daisy chuckled. "It will completely go to Millie's head."

"We'll take it slow."

Her gaze dropped to my lips.

"How slow?" she asked, barely above a whisper.

"Extremely."

Daisy nodded. "You do live in Madison."

"And you live in Buttercup Lake."

Without thinking, I leaned down and kissed her, tasting the maple syrup on her lips. She let out a little moan of approval as she leaned into me.

Her body fit perfectly in the harbor of mine, and the attraction only intensified.

Just when her lips parted and I thought I might explode, the doorbell rang.

Daisy stepped back with a dopey grin on her face while the chemicals swished around my bloodstream. I didn't want that kiss to end.

I wanted so much more.

The doorbell rang again, and Daisy shrugged. "Let's hope that's not Brielle."

Laughing, I shook my head as I made my way to the door.

I swung it open to see my parents standing in the hallway with their suitcases.

"The hotel screwed up our reservation," my Dad explained.

My mom's eyes narrowed on mine. "Since when did you start wearing hot pink lipstick?"

I traced my mouth with my fingers and wiped off the lipstick with a laugh as my mom craned her neck around me to see Daisy, and I knew this weekend just took a sudden turn.

Chapter Eleven

Daisy

The lips did not disappoint, and it took all my focus to stay upright and decent. My world spun into an incredible web of confusion as I reconciled the kiss with his parents showing up.

And my lipstick!

On his mouth.

"I thought I heard you might be down here working, Daisy. I'm so glad Hunter remembered his manners and invited you to stay here." His mom smiled at him. "And your sister said Brielle is calling again."

I snickered as I walked into the kitchen to do the dishes. I needed some sort of distraction from the kiss.

And his parents.

The water ran over the sticky pancake plates, and I got a strange satisfaction in watching the sugar dissolve.

It wasn't like I hadn't met his parents before. I'd met Hunter's mom several times through the book club and around town and his dad at a couple of celebrations.

I just never expected to have her son covered in my lipstick when she popped by his apartment unexpectedly.

"What's that all about with Brielle?" she asked. It became clear where Hunter got his directness, but I didn't mind at all because I wondered that, too.

Hunter didn't respond, so she smiled in my direction.

"How are you doing, Daisy?"

I turned around with a dishcloth in my hand and grinned. "Really good."

"Have you finished the chapters for book club?" she asked.

Definitely a recon mission.

I shook my head. "No. I was planning on doing that this afternoon before my shift."

His mom smiled wider and glanced at her son. "Why is she doing the dishes?"

Hunter's eyes connected with mine in a quick plea for help, and I grinned. He had his hands full, but I loved every second of it.

I could feel how much his parents loved him.

And then a thought occurred to me. If I were in the guest room, how was this going to work?

His parents walked over to the living room and took a seat on the couch facing the lake, and I motioned for Hunter to come into the kitchen.

"What's up?"

"With your parents here, I think I should stay at a hotel this weekend," I whispered.

"Nonsense," his mom yelled from the other room. "Hunter can sleep on the pull-out sofa here, and we will take Hunter's room."

Hunter rolled his eyes and grinned. "See? Problem solved."

"I love having the Christmas carols on," his mom continued, "but where are all your Christmas decorations?"

"Daisy already pointed that out. I'm headed out to grab a tree and anything else I can find."

His mom nodded. "Sounds like fun. We'll come with you."

I hid a smile as Hunter looked exasperated, and I

wiped down the counters. There was so little in life that got Hunter riled up. It was kind of fun to see.

"Help me," he whispered, squeezing my hands.

"Not me. I've got eight chapters to read and a bartending gig later."

"Fine. I'll remember that when you need to be bailed out.."

I smacked his behind with the dishcloth. "I'm sure you will."

"Did you want any coffee or juice?" Hunter asked.

"I'll take coffee." His mom glanced over her shoulder at us.

"Me too." His dad wrapped his arm around his wife.

I looked at Hunter and wandered into the living room. "It was really nice seeing you both again, but I'm going to go upstairs and get my reading done."

His mom looked disappointed. "Are you sure you can't come?"

The one thing I didn't want to do was intrude. His parents made the trip all the way down here, and I didn't need to interfere. Plus, the less time they spent with me, the less they could report back to Millie.

I knew how her mind worked, and the less information, the better.

His mom stood and gave me a hug. "You are truly incredible to put up with my son." She turned to him. "No offense."

"No, of course not. Why would there be?" he joked.

I stifled a laugh and hugged her back before making my way up the stairs. As soon as my foot hit the first step, Purrlock jumped off the couch and followed me up the stairs.

By the time I got to my room, I collapsed on the bed and daydreamed about our kiss.

It was absolutely divine. I didn't know if it was merely the magic of the season or my crazy fantasized expectations or that he actually had lips from heaven to melt me in place.

But whatever the reason, I wanted another.

I stayed on the bed, stretching my arms toward the pillows as the cat hopped up next to me and curled on my pillow.

Today felt surreal. I never expected to open up more to Hunter, and I certainly didn't expect a kiss.

As I forced myself to get out of bed, I walked over to my bag, rifling through it until I found the infamous book.

I thought about going into the bonus loft, but I knew I'd wind up eavesdropping more than reading, so I shut the door softly and curled on top of the bed.

The book started off fun and brisk. I immediately loved the premise, but I couldn't help but wonder why Millie had jumped on this book. Obviously, if Hunter and I were the next victims, choosing a book about a bar at Christmas seemed fitting. But beyond that, there were very few similarities.

I'd already managed to get to chapter four when Hunter knocked gently and popped his head into the room.

"We're headed out. Are you sure you don't want to join us? Please?"

I chuckled and shook my head. "Not a chance. You go have fun."

He tapped the wall and turned around. "If that's what we want to call it."

Hunter stopped and turned around slowly.

My eyes met his, and my belly dipped with anticipation.

"That kiss earlier…" His voice trailed off as warmth spread through me. "Was unlike anything I've ever experienced."

I smiled and nodded. "In a completely platonic way."

He laughed. "Absolutely."

Hunter walked down the hall, and I fell back onto the pillows, clutching my book and feeling like I was back in junior high, experiencing my first crush all over again.

There was something so refreshing about Hunter, and I felt like I could open up my soul to him and he wouldn't crush it.

I'd always prided myself on keeping things inside. Even my cousin Carter didn't know the depths of sadness and grief I still felt over the loss of my mom and brother.

Of course, he was smart enough to know how devastated I was, but I never let on that it hurt as much today as it did back then.

I was nineteen.

Barely a sophomore in college. My brother was a junior. We'd chosen different majors and different schools.

But none of that mattered the day they were taken from me.

I dropped out of school the next semester. My friends tried to convince me to stay, but I couldn't even stay strong enough to remain close to them. So, I picked myself up as best as I could and found a profession that allowed me to listen to people and smile.

I needed to smile more than anything. And there were days when it hurt more to smile than to cry, but I found my solace at Silver Ridge Resort in Washington, where I picked up the pieces and started again as a bartender.

But as the years went on, I realized I wanted something more.

And my aunt, uncle, and cousin were all out in Wisconsin.

I was ready for family again.

Albeit on my terms.

And Buttercup Lake was more than I could even ask for, with friendly people who were like family, festivals celebrating just about everything in the world, and a closeness that helped fill part of the void.

Maya and Nina had become close friends, and they both wound up with a Knox brother.

But Hunter was the best of all.

And the most misunderstood.

As I stared at the ceiling, my mind drifted to the possibility of a Mr. Right. Or was Hunter a Mr. Right Now? I just didn't know.

Whatever this was between us felt fresh... and right.

The problem was that I didn't know what the future held, and the future I'd always imagined got taken away from me.

And that left me scared and worried that I would always be faced with that kind of pain.

The sound of the front door closing below signaled

they'd left for their shopping right when my phone rang.

I glanced down to see Millie's name pop up.

"Hi, Millie."

"How'd you know it was me?"

"I have your smiling face pop up whenever it's your number."

"Oh, that's right." She chuckled. *"Anyway, I wanted to let you know that I spoke to your boss, and she's going to call you later."*

"Okay…" I wasn't sure where that was going.

"But I thought I'd let you know the good news. The smoke damage isn't as bad as they initially thought, so they're opening back up next weekend."

My heart unexpectedly took a plunge.

I'd just gotten here, and it was kind of fun.

"But that's not the reason I called. I was hoping that since you'll be back in town, I can count on you to make your fudge for the Sunshine Breakfast Club's Holiday Bazaar on Saturday."

"Uh, sure," I told her.

I'd totally forgotten about the bazaar.

"Why do you suddenly sound glum?" Millie asked.

I laughed, recognizing my mistake. Never show a weakness to a Sunshine Breakfast Club member. "I'm not glum at all."

Millie chuckled some more. "*And here I thought you might be disappointed that you're leaving Hunter early.*"

"Leaving Hunter? I'm not leaving Hunter. I'm leaving his bar early, but that has nothing to do with Hunter."

"*You two would make such a cute couple.*"

Boy, she was being far blunter about it than other times. Usually, she'd have people sneaking around, employing nefarious techniques to get things moving.

"Well, thanks. But I'm not in the market for a relationship."

"*Hogwash.*"

I laughed, shaking my head. "Pardon?"

"*You're just being scared.*"

"I'm not scared." I let out a slow breath. "Okay, I might be a little scared of falling for him, or anyone, really." I even kept my friendships at arm's length.

"*Have you ever baked a souffle?*" she asked.

"Yeah. Why? You want one of those for the bazaar too?"

"*No, but love is like a souffle. Sure, it has the potential to collapse, implode, or otherwise be an unpleasant experience, but what if...*"

"What if what?"

"*What if it doesn't? Think about the joy it brings when you see that sucker rising. It's growing until it's nearly weightless and carries you through life's hardships.*"

"Are you talking about the souffle any longer?"

"*This has nothing to do with Hunter, Daisy. But don't be afraid to love.*"

"I'll try to remember that." I glanced at the book. "And I'm four chapters into my reading assignment."

"*Perfect. You can Zoom in with us this week.*"

I chuckled. "I figured I wouldn't get out of it."

"*And one more thing, Daisy.*"

"Okay."

"*Hunter might be obnoxiously good-looking, but he has a heart of gold. Just like you. I know your uncle can't ever thank you enough for stopping everything you had going on in your life to help him out after his stroke.*"

"That's what family is for."

"*Not every family has someone like you, honey.*" She drew a breath. "*Do you know how Hunter wound up opening a bar in Madison?*"

"I just figured he liked the city."

"*He actually finished up business school down there and looked up tremendously to one of his professors.*"

My heart skipped a beat. There was so much more to

learn about Hunter, and I wanted to inhale it all.

"Yeah?"

"*And the professor had a bar that he ran, and Hunter worked there on the weekends and evenings.*"

I chuckled, thinking Hunter reminded me more of the partying type than the working type.

But who knew?

"*The professor got ill, and he didn't have any family, but Hunter did everything he could to help take care of him. Hunter almost didn't finish his degree, but he was determined to do it all. He'd help the professor, run the bar, and take his tests. His parents were worried sick about him.*"

"What happened to the professor?"

"*He passed three months after Hunter graduated, and Hunter inherited the bar.*"

A chill skated across my skin, even though I had blankets piled around me.

"I had no idea," I said quietly.

"*My point is that Hunter has felt tremendous loss, too. It doesn't compare to what you've been through, but he isn't someone who doesn't know how to care deeply.*"

My cheeks flushed, and I let out a deep breath. "I'll remember that."

"*And do enjoy the next few chapters. Jackson just got*

143

home with some pecan pie from that bakery that just opened up. I'll talk to you later."

"Thanks, Millie. Enjoy."

"Just remember, life can be like riding a rollercoaster with your eyes closed. There'll be moments where you scream, laugh, cry, and throw up, but at the end of the day, if you have someone's hand to hold, it makes everything better." She chuckled. *"And I'm not only talking about Hunter."*

"I appreciate that, Millie. I'll try to remind myself to be more open."

"That's all anyone can be. See you soon, dear."

Millie hung up, and I let out a deep sigh, wondering why Hunter never mentioned anything about the professor.

Chapter Twelve

Hunter

Daisy was undoubtedly part ballerina with a sprinkle of rockstar. Her delicate balance between Wonder Woman and Joan Jett confused people just enough to keep them guessing as she blazed through the orders. Some of the men wanted to flirt with her and did, while the women flocked to her and chatted about all of life's problems. She managed to keep everyone happy as she shook martinis and drew draft beers.

Being around her made my mind a whirlwind of mush and hope. I'd imagined flirty one-liners that would roll off my tongue while trying to impress her with rugged charm...

When all that would actually come out were a few grunts and a nod.

We'd been getting so close these last few days, but there was something different in the air tonight.

And the only thing I could blame it on was that brief kiss yesterday.

It was like the seriousness of what this could be hit us both hard.

There was the obvious physical attraction, but the emotional pull I felt to Daisy was on another level.

It felt insane to experience this type of connection, this inexplicable bond, and maybe that was why I stayed so far away last year.

I wouldn't really know what to do with it.

I still didn't.

Daisy's laughter rang through the bar, and her gaze met mine. I felt the familiar flutter as our eyes locked. She gave me a little wave with her fingers, charging the air with flirty electricity.

Did every man feel this lucky when she looked at them?

I pushed myself off the wall, feeling a restlessness in my bones.

We hadn't talked much since I'd left to go shopping

yesterday.

When it slowed down at the bar, I made my way over and sat down.

"Okay, Boss," she cooed with a playful tilt of her head. "What can I get you?"

"Club soda with ice."

Daisy grinned, reaching for a glass that she quickly filled with ice and poured the club soda over.

"I missed you yesterday," I told her. "It would have been nice to have some backup."

She smiled, crossing her arms over her chest. "What makes you think I'd be on your side?"

I laughed and shook my head. "Nothing now."

Daisy chuckled and leaned against the counter. Her hazel eyes glinted with mischief. "I got some news about the reopening of Styx."

My heart plummeted. "Yeah?"

"They're opening early. My boss was hoping I could come back for the weekend."

The news smacked into me like a physical blow to the chest. The thought of not getting to see her all the time and possibly losing the connection we'd built was almost unbearable.

Her words coiled around me, tightening their grip

with each pasting moment.

I didn't want Daisy to leave. I'd counted on two weeks.

But it wasn't my choice.

"I'll miss you," I said, gauging her reaction.

She grinned and reached for a rag to wipe the bar down. "I'm going to miss Purrlock a lot."

"The cat? That's who made an impression?"

A wry grin looped along Daisy's beautiful mouth. "Truth be told, I was just warming up to you too. I'm going to miss you. As a friend."

It felt like the rest of the bar drifted away as she watched me closely, probably waiting for me to say the right thing, but I didn't know what that could be. I was falling for Daisy, the real Daisy. Not just the woman I'd imagined as being fun and perky last year.

Rather, the woman whose layers were complex and who had a smile laced with a sadness few knew about.

But she chose me.

Daisy opened up to me and gave me a piece of herself that she'd shielded from so many.

A waitress came up to the bar and ordered a round of drinks for her table, which Daisy quickly worked on.

Now wasn't the time to talk to her about my feelings,

but I worried I wouldn't find the time. I'd always done well at avoiding those things. That's probably how I wound up with Brielle. I never talked about things, so she just assumed we were together. Then, one week turned to two months, and on and on.

But with Daisy, I wanted to be intentional. I wanted my actions to be deliberate, to mean something.

Like the kiss yesterday.

I looked around the familiar bar that had become my own. The twinkling lights strung along the bar cast a warm glow against the granite countertops.

The bar felt like home, especially during the holidays. It was the one place I could come to feel cheered up.

Daisy's eyes met mine as a new flood of orders came in. "I'd better get back at it."

I stood, leaning against the polished mahogany bar, watching Daisy as she effortlessly moved between patrons and waitresses, laughing or lending an ear.

Daisy had become the center of my universe without even trying, just like last year. It just snuck up on me.

Even though I'd owned the bar for years, there'd never been someone who had a presence like Daisy. She lit up the place, and her laughter was intoxicating.

But I knew this was all temporary.

I just hadn't expected only one week. My secret hope had been that it would take the bar up north longer to reopen.

Daisy flashed me a smile and cocked her head slightly when she realized I'd been contemplating things.

She mouthed three words, which took me by surprise. "Are you okay?"

I smiled, nodding.

It was moments like these where the nostalgia of everything came pressing down on me. This bar, my life, wouldn't have been possible if it weren't for my friend and professor who'd believed in me when I didn't even believe in myself.

But now, I wondered if there was more after this bar.

I glanced at Daisy again as she chatted with one of the patrons while handing him a drink, and I knew she was brightening that guy's night, too.

It wasn't that I had to be with Daisy all the time. It was just that my life was better when she was around.

As I did my duty, working the crowd and ensuring everything was up to the patrons' standards, I couldn't help but flash Daisy a look now and again.

And the thrill when I'd catch her looking back felt like I'd won the lottery.

The night wore on, and eventually, the customers

thinned enough to sit at the bar while Daisy finished up. Perry made his way over and leaned against the counter.

"Thank goodness you were here, Daisy. I wouldn't have been able to handle tonight by myself," Perry told her.

"It was fun." She glanced at me. "But I just found out this was my only weekend night here. The bar is opening back up, and I'm not on tomorrow."

Perry clutched his chest in dramatic fashion and groaned. "Please tell me that's not true."

I nodded slowly in agreement. "It's true. The bar isn't going to be the same without her."

Perry let out another sigh. "I swear my tips go up just by having you around, Daisy."

She chuckled. "You two know how to make a girl feel good."

Perry smiled, catching my gaze. "Just stating the truth."

"Well, thanks." She shrugged.

"I saw something got you down earlier," Perry said, tilting his head.

My heart skipped a beat. Where had I been? How did I not notice?

She shifted her weight from one foot to the other and let out a sigh. "Oh, just something one of the customers had said got to me. It was kind of sad."

"Happens this time of year. I like to say that I'm a licensed mixologist and therapist." Perry straightened and drew a breath. "Why don't you punch out and relax? I'll do the cleanup tonight."

Daisy shook her head. "I couldn't do that to you."

"You did it for me the other night. It's the least I could do."

"My feet are killing me," she confessed.

"Good. It's decided." I glanced at the corner of the bar. "Did you want to grab a cheeseburger or something?"

She chewed her bottom lip for a split second and nodded, her gaze landing on mine. "You don't mind?"

"Kitchen's still open," I said, smiling.

Perry gave me a nod and went to place the order for us.

We stole a corner booth toward the back of the bar. The low hum of Christmas music wafted through the air.

My eyes connected with hers. "Everything okay?"

She smiled and let her shoulders relax as she leaned against the booth. "Yeah. I just saw a mom and son at the bar. They were arguing about something so petty, and I had a flashback to my brother and mom. They got into a squabble right before they left the house." She laughed softly. "It was about the most ridiculous thing."

"Yeah? What about?"

She let out an exasperated sigh. "Where my brother wanted to spend New Year's." She traced her fingers along a napkin. Her gaze snapped to mine, and I felt that familiar pull swim through me. "Why are you so easy to talk to?"

A smile tugged on my lips, and I shrugged. "I didn't know I was."

Daisy nodded, glancing around the bar. "Did you always want to own a restaurant or bar when you grew up?" She used air quotes around *grew up*.

I chuckled. "Since we're using that term loosely…"

"You know what I mean."

No one had ever asked me that. I didn't even want to ask myself that.

I shook my head. "No. I didn't know what I wanted to do. I knew that I was great at throwing ragers."

Her brows shot up with a snort. "Ragers?"

"Keggers. College parties," I explained. "And I'd taken a business class and really connected with the professor. He thought my way of looking at business was unique."

Daisy nodded, her gaze not leaving mine. "That's incredible."

"He kind of saved me from myself. I was definitely

more concerned with partying than school." I shook my head. "So stupid and such a waste. If he hadn't hired me to work on my off-hours, I probably would have flunked out. He... uh... eventually got sick, and I helped take care of him and this place." I couldn't believe I was reliving this moment in my life.

"While in school," she said. "Millie mentioned something about that."

I smiled in surprise, shaking my head. "She did?"

"Yup."

"He was a good friend, a great mentor, and he surprisingly left me this bar. Honestly, all I've wanted to do since was make him proud. I miss him every single day."

Daisy nodded, reaching for my hands across the table. "I'm so sorry."

"It's kind of ironic, isn't it?"

"What's that?" she asked.

Perry brought over the cheeseburgers with fries for us, noticing Daisy's hands in mine.

"Thanks, Perry."

He nodded and wandered toward the bar as Daisy studied me. "It's ironic that we both share this connection, but it's somehow rooted in something we'd both rather not have."

"Loss," she whispered, letting out a sigh.

A twinge of pain shot through me. "Yeah."

"It's not just that, though, Hunter. There's more here." She brought her plate closer as empathy filled her gaze. "I know there is something special between us. I just don't know what it's supposed to be yet, do you?"

I smiled, knowing what I wanted it to be.

"I think it will become clearer with time."

She took a bite and nodded. "You're probably right." She took another bite and closed her eyes. "Best burgers ever."

"Thanks."

She opened her eyes, grinning. "You didn't cook it."

"Ouch." I chuckled.

"Thanks for sharing that with me about your friend."

"I couldn't think of anyone else I'd rather share it with," I confided.

"What was his name?"

"Professor Thomas."

"He sounds like a smart man." She smiled, her hand reaching out to softly brush mine. "You're talented at what you do here. I can tell people love it here. He'd be very proud."

I nodded, realizing grief was like a maze of dead ends until one day, someone helped clear the path.

Chapter Thirteen

Daisy

"Hey, Hunter," Evie called out through the crowd. I spotted her immediately, rushing past the gigantic Christmas tree waiting to be lit at the ceremony.

"Is that my sister?" Hunter scanned the deluge of people as Beckett and Cash towered through the crowd. Their sister stood about six inches shorter than her brothers and appeared ecstatic to see Hunter. "What a surprise."

She dashed toward him, and he swung her around before setting her back down. Maya and Nina waved at me while I took in this family reunion. It felt really nice to be surrounded by such a strong family unit. I had that with my cousin and his family, but this somehow pulled me into their orbit.

"Surprise," his mom said from behind. "We thought whatever was going on tonight deserved getting your siblings here too. And since Evie just flew in, it's perfect timing."

"This is awesome." He glanced at me, and I saw a fleck of embarrassment dash through his gaze. "But honestly, tonight isn't that big of a deal."

She laughed, giving me a squeeze before making her way to her daughter. "Well, that's what happens when you're cryptic and only tell me parts of your plans."

A shiver ran through me as the wind picked up. Hunter noticed and draped his arm around my shoulders. I spotted a children's choir filing onto the stage next to the Christmas tree and glanced at Hunter, wondering what made this night so special for him.

Cash clapped his hands together and blew into them. "This had better be good, Hunter. This was a long drive."

Maya elbowed his brother and chuckled. "Be nice."

Everything seemed so easy with this crew. It felt the same way when I was with Hunter, too.

Things were effortless.

But maybe that was because we weren't in a

relationship. We were platonic, with an accidental kiss thrown into the mix.

Our dating history kept turning into a mingle of maybes and almosts. There was absolutely nothing definite about any of this.

I drew a breath and watched the mayor make her way onto the stage as the kids started singing *O Holy Night*. I looked at Hunter's mom, who was leaning her head against his dad, swaying to the music. Cash brought Maya into his arms, and Beckett looped his arm around Nina's waist.

Hunter's eyes connected with mine, and he pulled me in closer, placing a whisper of a kiss on top of my head.

The only thing that would make tonight more magical was if snow started falling. I reached up and looped my fingers through Hunter's as he kept his arm draped over my shoulders. I scanned the crowd, taking in all the families, some singing along with the carols while others patiently waited for the tree lighting ceremony.

As the choir wound down, the mayor stepped up to the microphone. "Tonight, we are here to celebrate a wonderful time of the year where neighbors can slow down a little to say hi or offer a cup of cheer, and bosses can remember that their businesses wouldn't survive without their employees and that kindness goes a long way. And on that note, I'd like to welcome Hunter Knox up here to say a few words. He was kind enough to sponsor this year's tree lighting and to donate one hundred thousand dollars to the Children's Hospital here in Madison."

The crowd cheered as Hunter swept a kiss along my cheek and made his way up to the stage. His mom squeezed her husband's hand and whispered, "He did?"

His dad chuckled and proudly smiled at his son.

"Thank you all for being here. I'll keep this brief since the temperature is dropping by the second. The holidays are a time to reflect, embrace, and dream about the new year. While the twinkling lights are beautiful, the true essence of this holiday comes from sharing our love with others, providing joy for those who can't quite find it, and weaving a world that is united, even if only in our tiny communities. Let us cherish these moments with family and friends this holiday season and know that these memories will stay with us long after the season has passed. Let's extend our hands and hearts to those who quietly struggle and bring compassion to those in need this holiday season and beyond. Thanks, everyone, for coming out. Now, let's light this tree."

Hunter's gaze locked on mine, and he waved me up onto the stage as the mayor began a countdown from ten. Maya and Nina pushed me through the crowd as the numbers dwindled. Hunter hopped down a couple of steps and helped me on stage as the crowd shouted down from two and then one.

The Christmas tree's red and white sparkling lights flickered majestically as the children's choir belted out *Deck the Halls*.

Hunter smiled, taking me in as he slid his arm around my waist, and we admired the Christmas tree.

The mayor came over, thanking Hunter for his generosity, and I felt true pride in knowing this man. Hunter's parents walked over with his siblings as we turned and left the stage. Evie threw herself at her brother and chuckled. "I knew you were a good guy."

His dad's lip curled. "Always doing the right thing. That's my boy."

Hunter chuckled. "I like to surprise you when you least expect it."

Cash nodded. "This was definitely worth the drive. I'm really proud of you."

A hot chocolate stand opened up across the lawn, where several lines snaked around the stage. A hot dog cart had a line nearly as long.

"You guys hungry?" Hunter asked. "I know a place that has pretty good food and cheap drinks."

"But is your beer as good as my gingerbread beer?" Cash asked.

Hunter eyed me as I kept in a snicker. "Just different is all."

"Maya says I still have to perfect it, but I think I'm getting pretty close."

Hunter linked his fingers with mine as we waited at the crosswalk. His bar was only down a block from the park. As we walked toward the building, I glanced around his family.

I didn't know where I fit in. They certainly made me feel easy about things and accepted, but I didn't know my place. At times, it felt like what Hunter and I shared was more intimate than just friends, but then this wall would come up.

But I didn't know if the wall was from him or me or both of us.

When we made it to the bar, Hunter opened the door, and we all rushed in, shivering to get the blood flowing again.

Perry spotted us and gave a quick wave. "How did the lighting go?"

"Amazing," his mom gushed. "I'm so proud of my son."

Perry nodded. "Did the mayor announce your donation?"

Hunter nodded. "She did. I'd asked her not to."

Perry laughed. "And I asked her to make sure she did." Perry glanced at us. "My son became very sick last year, and while we had good medical, the bills still took a toll. Hunter was right there by our family's side. I'd say he spent almost as much time with my little guy as we did."

Hunter's mom studied her son as if she'd never known this side of him existed.

But I knew.

The professor knew.

"He's an amazing little boy," Hunter said, shaking his head. "I'm just glad things worked out well."

"Anyway," Perry continued despite Hunter's warning look, "he got really chummy with the staff there and still volunteers, but this year, he did something that touched our family's heart so much."

I watched Hunter's reaction as his friend and employee bragged about him. It was a cross between irritation and unease.

"He donated that money in honor of our son, specifically to cover costs for families who can't afford the treatment needed." Perry grinned. "I'm proud to work at a place with an owner like that."

His brothers stared at Hunter like he'd grown an extra

head, but pride weaved throughout everyone.

"I don't want all this going to my head," Hunter said, laughing. "But thanks, Perry."

Perry grinned as Hunter led us to a table overlooking the city sidewalk. He slid two tables together, and everyone got situated while Perry brought the menus.

When everyone found their seat, Hunter cleared his throat and laughed. "Had I known all that other stuff was going to be mentioned, I wouldn't have invited you."

His dad laughed. "Figures, but I'm really proud of you."

Beckett laughed. "The frat boy has grown up."

Hunter glared at his brother as only siblings did.

"This is an amazing impromptu family reunion," his mom said, completely giddy.

I looked around the table, feeling at home and hoping that when I returned to Buttercup Lake, I'd still be a part of this somehow.

Even as it was now.

As Hunter's friend.

"I heard you're coming back up north sooner than you expected," his mom said, looking at me over the menu. "Hunter, are you going to miss your housemate?"

Evie eyed her brother, and he nodded.

"Daisy is an amazing roommate." He slid his hand onto my knee and gently squeezed it.

"And Daisy is kind enough to share her lipstick with him," his dad revealed.

My cheeks flushed a million shades of pink while laughing with everyone.

"Well, we're so happy to have you dating our brother," Cash explained, and my eyes widened.

I quickly shook my head. "Oh, we're not dating. We're just—"

"We're just friends." Hunter grinned as platters of appetizers came out to the table, with Perry and Michelle delivering them.

Perry rolled his eyes, and I laughed.

Had he picked up on the connection Hunter and I had, too?

Or was I just flirting so obviously that it couldn't be ignored?

"Oh, right." Beckett's wry grin only widened as he looked at Cash. "The old *just friends* trick."

"It's true," I protested. "We're both realists. He lives hours away, and I'm completely incapable of relationships, so friends it is."

"We'll see about that," his mom muttered, and I

snickered. "It's true, Daisy. You're an absolute sweetheart with enough fire in you to keep Hunter in line."

I laughed, absorbing all the compliments while shaking my head. "There is no keeping Hunter in line."

"Very true," Evie said, pointing her fork at me with a cheese curd on the tip. "Knowing that, you'll fit right in with the family."

"Guys, let's not scare her off." Hunter's gaze locked on mine, and that's when I knew he'd never be able to.

Until his phone buzzed and Brielle announced she'd be in town and would be stopping by the bar in four days.

It was like that bit of news ripped away all the good cheer I'd managed to bottle up, and now, I wanted nothing more than to go back home to Buttercup Lake and start my holidays over.

Chapter Fourteen

Hunter

This wasn't the ending I'd expected for tonight. Brielle had a real knack, and I was at the point of wanting to block her, but there was something extremely persistent about her tactics that had me worried. After all of my family had left for their drive back to Buttercup Lake, I texted a quick *Fine* to Brielle and hoped that whatever she wanted to talk about would just end on that day.

Daisy became quiet the moment she saw the text pop up on my phone, and I didn't blame her.

What was starting between her and me was special. She knew it, and I knew it.

And I shouldn't be having random messages from an ex continually popping up, but they were.

Daisy and I had come back to my place, and she immediately wandered to the Christmas tree, admiring the ornaments that my mom had helped me with.

She gasped when her fingers fell to the one I'd hoped she'd see.

"Hunter, how did you get this?" Her eyes flew back to the ornament that was the photo of her flipping a pancake.

I laughed. "Hallmark has just about everything, and I got the photo done at the one-hour photo next to it. I can be pretty ingenious when it's important."

Her eyes connected to mine, and she nodded. "I see that, and I'm flattered."

I slowly walked toward Daisy, feeling the connection between us only getting stronger.

"I'm sorry about that text popping up."

She shrugged and turned her gaze back to the tree. "It's okay."

"No, it's really not."

I slowly traced my arms around her waist and turned her toward me. "I want you to know that I'm falling for you, Daisy. Hell, I've already fallen for you. I'm past that now. There isn't a second that goes by when I'm not thinking about

167

you."

"Hunter," she whispered, cupping her hands on my chest. "I'm scared of losing you."

Daisy's words dug deep into my soul. They weren't just frivolous words. She meant it. She'd forever lost the two people she cared about most in this world.

She wasn't worried that I'd just go away and not talk to her. She was worried about the greatest kind of pain.

Loss.

"All we can promise each other is our own forever," I said softly. "But I don't want you to be afraid with me, Daisy. We can learn, grow, and imagine our own futures. Together."

A tiny smile curved onto her lips, and she let out a wistful sigh. "Then I want to spend as much time together as we can... learning."

"I can do that."

She was quiet for a few minutes. "It's been so long since I've let myself feel anything for anyone. I've just been numb, grieving, and drifting privately while outwardly looking like I've got it all together. But it's been years like this, Hunter. I even managed to figure out a way to keep friendships on my outer periphery." She let out another breath. "But with you, I feel every ounce of living. You surprised me with your kindness and thoughtfulness. You let me feel at my own pace. You don't push me beyond where I want to go."

Her words socked me right in the gut. She was so torn up about her past, and it was distorting her idea of a future.

"It's because I know what this can be. I know what we have can be really special if we let it."

Daisy nodded and brought her eyes to mine as I pulled her closer. "Me too, and that scares me more than anything. I haven't felt this vulnerable… ever."

"I'll always be here for you. No matter what." I ran my hands along her spine, and a little shiver passed through her. "Even if or when you tell me to go fly a kite."

She giggled, and the sound made my entire body respond. I wanted to know what it felt like to be one with her, have her body curl around mine, hold her, feel her, taste her.

My body ached to have this woman.

Daisy slowly traced her fingers up my arms and drew a deep breath. "I want to feel what it's like to be loved by you. I want you…" Her voice trailed off, and I realized there wasn't more for her to say. She'd said it.

"I want you, Daisy."

"Tonight," she added with a smile.

The magnetic pull on Daisy only worsened. If we did this, there would be no going back. I knew it. She knew it. The force between us was too powerful to pretend it didn't exist.

For a year, I'd beaten myself up for messing up my chance to be with her, and now, she was handing me one last chance.

I wasn't going to screw it up.

Her hands skated along my chest as her big, hazel eyes studied me.

The frenzied desire running between us was indescribable. I'd never felt anything like it before. My left hand cupped her head while my right ran along her back, pulling her into me.

Her breathing quickened as her eyes turned feverish with need. She pressed her body harder against me, and I smiled, taking her in.

A few stray hairs had fallen from her braid, framing her face. Her eyes gleamed with the same restless desire running through me.

Daisy's hands moved to my hips, feeling my hardness as her breath caught.

"You're so beautiful," I whispered.

She tilted her head slightly, and my mouth collided with hers. She let out a little moan of goodness as she angled her chin slightly, parting her mouth and letting me taste the sweetness of her lips.

I wanted so much more. I could feel her body pressing harder and harder against me as our kisses intensified. My fingers tangled through her hair as her hands ran under my sweater. The softness of her hands feathering over my bare skin made me so hard it hurt.

Her hands teased me as our kisses quickened with a frantic need that was building between us. It felt like all of our confessions, dreams, and thoughts tangled into this kiss as my body reacted to her.

Daisy's tongue slid between my lips, teasing, taunting, and welcoming me into hers. The way her kiss deepened, her little whimpers buzzing through me, was nearly unbearable.

As if we were so deeply connected, she slowly rolled her tongue with mine and slowed our kisses. Her head leaned to the side as her breathing quickened, exposing her neck. I kissed along the bare skin, smelling the vanilla I'd always loved.

Her fingers tangled through my hair, pulling me closer as my tongue tasted her sweetness before raising my head to kiss her again.

Minutes went by that felt like seconds, and I knew I had to get her to my bedroom. The need to be inside her only grew with every passing moment.

As if sensing the next steps, Daisy's lips parted from mine, and she drew a breath, her gaze glassy with the same desire I felt.

She shook her head slowly, and my heart dropped. She'd always been a bundle of contradictions, but this pause I didn't understand. Did she change her mind?

Her eyes stayed on mine as my heart raced and my breathing stayed ragged. I saw the storm of emotion roiling through her gaze. She was so outwardly kind, caring, and a free spirit. Inwardly, she was so vulnerable. I refused to say fragile because she was the strongest woman I'd met, but in this second, I detected a delicate emotional turmoil running through her.

Our connection wasn't about lust and one-night stands. The bond we'd been building had been constructed from the heartache that grew into comfort from each other and the ease of sharing life's memories and dreams.

But we could only do that if we let our walls down. If she let her walls down.

"Daisy, developing love isn't only about the good times. There will be difficulties and hardships ahead. That's life, but I promise you, it gets easier when you have someone to share it with. I saw that between my parents."

And that's when I realized what I'd said.

Love.

She cupped her hand around my neck and nodded. "I know love is possible with you, Hunter. That's what scares me. I want to be able to love you fiercely without holding back." She flashed a crooked smile. "And this is my first step." She glanced around the living room and grinned. "Now, take me upstairs. There are too many windows."

Chapter Fifteen

Daisy

I settled into his embrace while a waterfall of emotions washed over me. He was like a powerful current sweeping me up in a collision of emotions, but I couldn't shake the worry of losing him.

That had always been my worry about Hunter Knox. He was good-looking, confident, successful, and sure of things. But I wasn't sure of much. I only knew how badly it hurt to lose the people I loved. Maybe all those times I'd dreamed about kissing Hunter had been my way of keeping the walls up because I didn't dare to dream of something more

174

with him.

To have him lift the curtains to see my true self, not the one I always showed to everyone else.

But in his strong and protective arms, he felt like the safest place in the world.

This intimate space.

His bedroom.

Everything felt more profound, more real.

My mind was trapped in a torrent of raw emotions and spiraling thoughts. I'd fallen for him like the winter storm outside. The swift, unexpected, and overwhelming sensations crashed into me and made his embrace even more of a sanctuary.

But I worried that it was merely the magic of the holidays weaving this spell around us.

Hunter ran his arms around my waist, and his eyes connected with mine, sending a jolt of electricity clear to my toes. There was something so raw and demanding about the way he looked at me. His eyes held such depth and affection that I'd finally felt cherished in life. His adoration shone bright and clear like the star atop his Christmas tree.

I giggled, which made a smile roll onto his lips.

"I know it's been a while for me, but am I that comical?" he teased, smoothing his hands along my hair.

175

I shook my head, smiling. "Not at all. I'm just suddenly swallowed up by holiday metaphors. Everything just feels so… special."

We stood at the foot of his bed.

I couldn't help but think about how hard I'd fallen for him. The connection we shared was unexpected, powerful, and all-consuming. Every moment with him seemed to deepen our relationship, and the thought of surrendering my heart, soul, and body to him was exhilarating and scary.

Because there was no going back.

So far, things had been easy. This intense bond that had formed between us meant so much, but I couldn't deny his magnetic presence. Hunter's irresistible force was like a magnet that might skew my reality.

Hunter smiled and drew a deep breath as he pulled my head down to kiss me, and his other hand found my butt, bringing me closer to him. The power in his grip made the heat in my belly hotter as my desire for him only intensified.

His kisses tasted so good. His lips were so soft, but his mouth was demanding. It was like every cell in my body ignited with a fierce craving for him.

I dipped my hand into his jeans, feeling down the treasure trail until I wrapped my fingers around him.

His breath hitched against my lips as I gripped him

firmly and unzipped his jeans with my other hand.

"Daisy," he whispered between kisses as he lifted me onto the bed, my hands still feeling him in my grip.

He moved his fingers under my sweater, gliding along my skin and creating a flutter of butterflies. The desire to feel him inside me outweighed all common sense. Nothing else mattered in this magical moment, and the thought of giving myself to him without reservation filled me with a thrilling sensation. I wanted to experience everything with him.

Working the clasp of my bra with one hand while his other expertly moved along my body created an intense frenzy of need. I'd always daydreamed about being kissed by Hunter, but this was extraordinary.

Hunter tugged my sweater over my head as I slid my hands along his chiseled abdomen before I worked my bra off. It fell to the floor as he pulled his jeans down. I reached for his briefs and pushed them down as a smile spread across Hunter's expression. His eyes canvassed down my body as I wiggled my hips to work my pants down.

"Daisy, you're what dreams are made of." His voice was gruff, but his touch was so tender as he moved over me.

His mouth sealed along my nipple with gentle teasing as his other hand worked down my thigh, coming to the warmth between my legs.

"I think I might be ready," I teased.

Hunter lifted his head and laughed, nuzzling my nose before kissing me again. His touch was gentle yet firm. His moves were a perfect balance that sent shivers down my spine.

The vulnerability of the moment was unmistakable. I turned over onto my stomach and glanced over my shoulder as his smile widened, bringing his gaze to mine. He slowly worked his hands down my spine, sending a shiver of anticipation through me. His fingers were replaced with his mouth, the dampness of his tongue gliding along my spine as I felt his body against mine.

"Hunter," I whispered as his other hand slid around me between my thighs. "You're incredible."

Hunter shook his head as his gaze stormed with need. He flipped me back over, and a shudder of anticipation shot through me. The need between us was insatiable.

In his embrace, I felt a profound sense of belonging and comfort. The hormones were racing through me, but it was more than just a physical attraction between us. Our minds and bodies were connected through our hearts. We were taking down our walls brick by brick, and the troubles from the outside world could wait. Right now, it was just us, and that was all that mattered.

Hunter's gaze locked on mine as he slid inside me.

His fullness expanded me almost to the brink as I closed my eyes in ecstasy, allowing myself to sink deeper into the feelings that surrounded us. His breathing quickened with every thrust. My breaths came faster as I tightened around him, my head lolling in extreme passion. I'd never felt anything like this.

Hunter's breaths came faster and harder as my world shattered into a complex roar of emotions. His deep moan melted into me as I felt our bodies collide.

It was okay to finally let go. What we'd shared was a beautiful, complex mix of love and longing to be heard.

His breathing was ragged as my legs wrapped around his waist, and his eyes steadied on mine. "I've never…"

I nodded, cutting him off. "Same."

He brought me into his arms, kissing me along my neck and back to my mouth.

To be this physically and emotionally close exhilarated me, but I couldn't help but feel a little dread. What if I lost him too?

But as I listened to the steady beat of his heart, a sense of peace washed over me. It was as if every pump echoed a silent promise of hope, respect, and warmth.

Hunter propped himself on his elbows, his eyes searching mine as our worlds had totally combined. The intense warmth in his gaze made me feel cherished and wanted. His expression spoke volumes, but when his mouth pressed to mine again, I knew the magic of the season only enhanced what we already knew. We were falling in love.

I lay in his arms, thinking about all the hopes and dreams that were developing within me. I secretly hoped for a future with Hunter. And like he'd said, there would always be moments of joy along with distinct challenges, but if we were together, we'd be stronger.

"I think I'm falling in love with you, Hunter," I whispered.

"Then maybe I can finally stop hoping and wishing." He smiled. "My plan is finally working." He growled in my ear before peppering more kisses along my body.

"What plan was that?"

"To have you by Christmas. I told you hope was a powerful thing."

I closed my eyes, savoring the warmth of his lips against me, sinking deeper into the emotions that wrapped around us. Love, desire, hope—they all entwined, creating a tapestry of emotions that built my safe haven for the first time in... forever.

Chapter Sixteen

Hunter

The relentless voice in my head made me second-guess Daisy's intentions. Maybe she really did just need someone to talk to without feeling like there was an ulterior motive. But there was more to it than that. We both felt it.

Yesterday, after Daisy left, my brain wouldn't stop spinning. It was like one minute, our attraction sparked hotter than ever, zinging each of us with electricity we couldn't explain, and then the next, it turned into a complete friend zone.

She was really hard to read.

I thought about messaging her today, but I wasn't sure

she wanted to hear from me, especially after she heard about Brielle wanting to stop by the bar.

I'd put my foot down with Brielle, but she persisted in coming by the bar tonight.

Which had me concerned.

And it obviously didn't sit well with Daisy, which also hinted at her feelings being more than just friends.

But the kicker was that from the moment Daisy left, her departure made me want to hop in my car and drive to Buttercup Lake for the rest of the holidays. It wasn't like I'd plan some grand, romantic gesture to fall into the Sunshine Breakfast Club's clutches. Besides, I think Daisy would be turned off by that at this point, but every nagging thought I had felt like a bee buzzing incessantly in my ear, and it always led back to Daisy.

I'd let Brielle come tonight since I didn't have much choice there, hear what she had to say, and then I could just drive up to see Daisy for a quick trip.

So, really, I'd get more peace driving up north than staying here. Michelle could handle everything. We'd already talked about it.

I chuckled, shaking my head to the realization that Daisy truly had managed to get me all twisted up. My brothers always teased me and told me this would happen one day.

To them, it was proof that Brielle wasn't the one.

I knew she wasn't for a variety of reasons, but with Daisy, I saw a future. Things just fit.

Brielle always made me think I was walking on a tightrope, suspended high above a moat full of snapping crocodiles, and she was a crocodile. We never clicked. And I should have ended things with her long ago, but I wanted to give her a chance.

None of it mattered now. I just needed to get through the day and text Daisy to see if she'd be up for a visit.

Things had been casual so far, but I wasn't sure I still wanted to play that game.

In fact, I didn't want to play any game.

I grabbed myself a Coke and stared at my laptop, going over the last week's sales. They'd risen eleven percent.

Perry walked over and scooted a stool out next to me to eat his dinner before his shift started.

He took a bite of his patty melt and glanced at me. "You miss her?"

I laughed, shaking my head. "Not you, too."

"It's obvious, man. You two fit like two pieces of a puzzle."

"Is that so?"

He nodded, taking another bite.

"Daisy's a walking, talking contradiction." I shook my head. "We do good together, but I just don't want to scare her away."

"One thing I've learned is the easiest way to scare off someone you love is to not love hard enough. I learned it the hard way early on when I was dating Mary."

I nodded, listening to his advice. It made sense.

Perry held up his hand. "And I'm not saying you're in love. I'm just saying, be open. Let those emotions go where they may."

I shook my head, snagging a fry from his plate. "Even her laugh, Perry. I remember the first time I saw her. I'd gone up to Buttercup Lake for some family function, and of course, Brielle was with me."

"Ooh." Perry whistled. "Enough said."

I chuckled. "I just remember seeing Daisy and thinking I couldn't even talk straight or gather my thoughts up. Next thing I know, Millie and my mom are suggesting I hire Daisy temporarily, and I could barely remember I even had a bar."

Perry chuckled. "You acted like a complete goober last year when she came down to work. I'm glad you lightened up on her."

I grimaced. "That's another thing I worry about. I

don't want her to think that's who I am."

"She knows better."

"Hope so." I looked around the bar, which was beginning to fill up. The place usually felt like home, but all I could think about was getting up to Buttercup Lake.

I didn't know what Brielle wanted to tell me, but I prayed that it wasn't like every other time she'd begged her way back into my life. It was a brutal cycle.

"Brielle is stopping by."

"Excuse me?" Perry couldn't hide his shock. "You're gushing about Daisy, and now you're telling me Brielle is stopping by? How does that even work?"

"She's been calling and texting. She says she really needs to tell me something. She even left a message on my sister's phone. My hope is that I'm not just falling for one of her schemes."

"Wow. I didn't expect this."

"It's not ideal. I've put that long and windy chapter behind me, but the book just won't close." I clasped my hands together, wringing them nervously at the thought. "She wanted to stop by the apartment, but I told her it was here or nowhere."

Perry shook his head, wiping his hand along his chin. "I don't know what to say about that other than I'm glad it's you and not me."

I laughed, shaking my head. "I'm glad I can be that reminder for you about how awful it is to be single."

Perry stood, grinning. "No doubt. I'll be at the bar if you need me."

I nodded, sliding my phone out of my pocket and debating whether I should text Daisy.

I opened up the texts, and just seeing Daisy's picture on her profile made my world seem steady again. Her gorgeous smile hinted at something only she knew and held close to her.

Ah, what the heck. It's the holidays.

My fingers couldn't keep up with my thoughts.

Hey, Daisy. I've been thinking about you nonstop. I miss having you at the apartment, and Purrlock won't even look at me as if it's my fault you left. I was thinking maybe you'd be up for a visit. I thought about heading up to Buttercup Lake tomorrow. No pressure. But those are my plans.

I stared at the screen.

Did that sound like I was at all interested? *Or maybe I was too interested?*

"Hunter." Brielle's brisk voice grated over me as my finger accidentally hit *Send*.

I spun on the stool to see my ex standing behind me with her slender arms folded over her chest, her dark brows raised to inhumanly possible heights, and her lips already curled into a scowl.

Merry Christmas to me.

"Hey, Brielle. You're early."

Her gaze stayed on mine, and she gave a quick nod.

"Did you want to get a table by the window? It's probably a little more private."

"That would be fine." Her slim jeans accentuated her small waist, and the oversized sweater provided the only softness about her.

She followed me to a small table in the corner overlooking the bustling sidewalk. It didn't hurt that my bar's location was nestled among some great boutiques.

Brielle sat down and watched me pull out a chair and do the same.

"I don't know how to say this, but I think being direct is the best."

I dreaded what she was about to say. Usually, when she wanted to get back with me, she at least faked some sweetness, but today was void of that.

187

I nodded. "Absolutely. Brielle, I've moved on with my life. I'm content being alone. I like visiting my family up north more. I honestly don't know why you reached out again after so long. Aren't you happy with Nick?"

"Extremely." She eyed me. "But that's not why I'm here."

"Okay, enlighten me."

"Nick's schedule is extremely unpredictable and leads us overseas more often than not."

I nodded. "That sounds like your dream come true."

Travel had always been a point of contention between us. If she could spend all her time anywhere but here, she'd be thrilled. It looked like she'd found her perfect partner.

"It's fabulous. His apartment in Milan is to die for."

I chuckled. "Don't go doing that. So, what brought you back to Wisconsin? Isn't Chicago where your base is?"

"It is, but we're home for the holidays. His mom isn't doing very well, and the doctors advised her not to travel. We'd planned on spending Christmas in the Alps."

I detected Brielle's aggravation at his mother for being ill. It brought me right back to how she ran our relationship. If her plans didn't go precisely as she'd imagined, all hell would break loose.

"I'm sorry to hear about his mother. But I don't know

what any of this has to do with me."

Perry slowly walked over, bringing some water for us. He left as quietly as he came.

"I have a son," she said, analyzing my reaction.

"That's amazing, Brielle. Congratulations. I'm sure you make a great mom."

She shrugged. "I try, but I'm sure the nannies do better."

I wasn't sure what to say to that, so I just nodded and took a sip of water.

"I'm really happy for you."

She let out a sigh. "Here's the thing…"

I stared at Brielle as she nervously looked around the bar, and my heart started pounding for no reason.

"Nick and I started dating right after we broke up."

Which was code that she was seeing him while we were still together.

"Well, pregnancies are like that. They can sneak right up on a couple."

Her eyes darted to mine, and she nodded. "Maybe it would be better if I show you."

Being that I had no idea where she was going with this visit, I just nodded.

She slipped her phone out of her purse and tapped the

screen a few times.

"Nick has been a doll about the entire thing." She shook her head. "A truly phenomenal fiancé."

News to me, but congrats to her. I glanced at her ring finger and couldn't believe I hadn't noticed the whopping diamond on her finger.

"Congratulations on your engagement, but I'm sure he's thrilled he has a son."

She pursed her lips together and shook her head. "That's the thing. It's not his."

Brielle placed her phone in front of me, and I looked down at the baby boy.

Goosebumps peppered over me as I stared into the little guy's eyes.

They were shaped like...

Mine.

And his nose looked like mine when I was a baby, and the strong brow line. My pulse quickened as I stared at the phone as her finger swiped to the next photo. She didn't have to tell me for me to know.

An overwhelming amount of confusion swept through me.

"I don't understand."

"We thought I was pregnant with Nick's baby. But

after I had him, Nick started questioning me more about our timeline. You know, Nick has red hair, green eyes, and is so fair."

I drew a breath.

"And you clearly do not."

"What are you telling me?"

"Nick wasn't upset about it, but he did want me to do a DNA test."

I leaned into the table, waiting for her to say it.

But I already knew.

I had a son.

"The test proved that Nick wasn't the father, and I'd only slept with you and Nick."

My body warmed with something I hadn't expected.

Curiosity.

Love.

Yearning.

"And you can just tell by looking." She laughed.

"I'm in shock."

She nodded. "I bet."

"What's his name?"

"Tate."

I smiled, looking at the next picture of him. "He's adorable." I looked up at Brielle. "He's actually the cutest baby out there."

She finally cracked a smile. "Tate is a handful. He reminds me of you."

"Where is he? I'd like to meet him."

"Back at the hotel with the nannies."

"I just… I just need a second to regroup." I stared at the photo of Tate.

"I don't know how much you want to be involved…" Her voice trailed off.

"Fully. I want to be there every second." Realizing that wasn't possible, I shook my head. "As often as possible."

"I don't think we need to be flying all around with Tate. There are times I just don't see it being feasible to take him with us. I mean, there are several trips I've already missed out on."

Her words shook my core and were a stark reminder of Brielle. How could she not want him with her?

I looked at Tate, knowing there wasn't a single thing nearly as important as him, and I would do everything in my power to make him know that.

Chapter Seventeen

Daisy

There was nothing like being back home in Buttercup Lake. The week I'd been away had turned the town into a winter wonderland.

All the little storefronts had their Christmas decorations out, and my go-to coffee shop had brought back my favorite holiday drink called the Rudolph, which was white chocolate, cinnamon, and three shots of espresso with a dollop of gingerbread cold foam with a cherry on top.

It made up for the weather dropping to sixteen degrees this morning. All I had to do was remind myself that Madison's balmy temp of twenty-two didn't have a drink like this that could compete.

Even after all that goodness and loving being back here, I had to come to the stark realization that I missed Purrlock and Hunter.

Especially Hunter.

And with the text he'd sent me, it was safe to say he missed me too.

Which was good and confusing, a sort of confusing good that left open possibilities for our continued friendship.

But it left me wanting to start doing air quotes around friendship.

The more I thought about it and relived being in his arms, I knew there was nothing casual about what was happening.

Even his kisses worked magic on me, and my friends didn't experience things like that. They didn't walk away, barely able to stay upright with lips tingling for hours after, mind foggy, and having heart palpitations.

I had to admit to myself that I was falling for Hunter Knox. That was the first step.

I didn't know what the second step might be, but at least I had step number one figured out.

After he wrote me that text, I quickly wrote back that I'd have a roast waiting for him. I never heard back, but I assumed he got busy with the bar.

My only goal for the day was to stay awake and not become delirious from the lack of sleep I'd had from making fudge all night.

As I stepped inside the cozy antique store, the smell of sweet cider drifted around me, and I immediately spotted Maya. She wandered over with a big grin. "How are you this fine day?"

I chuckled, loosening my scarf. "Good, but you seem awfully chipper."

"I just found out some huge news." She grinned from ear to ear.

My brows quirked. "What's that?"

"My sister is pregnant again."

"Grace? Is that possible? Didn't she just have her little girl?"

She snickered. "That's what Jackson said, too."

I smiled, knowing how much Jackson loved his wife. My cousin had met his soul mate. No doubt about it.

"But I know Grace wanted to tell you herself, so act surprised."

I chuckled and nodded. "Is Izzy ecstatic?"

Grace's teenage daughter, Izzy, from Grace's first marriage, absolutely loved being a big sister for the most part.

"I think it makes her relieved to be going to college in a couple of years." She smiled. "But I think she's secretly excited, just showing it how some teenagers do." She wandered over to the counter where a carafe sat and poured herself some hot cider. "So, I'm just filling in while Grace gets some rest. Cider?"

"Sure." I chuckled, nodding. "Well, I spotted an old Spode ceramic Christmas ornament with a white cat a couple of weeks ago. I'm not sure if you still have it, but it reminds me of someone."

She walked over with my own paper cup of spiced cider. "I think I know the one."

I drifted toward the tree where I'd seen it a couple of weeks ago. "Ah-ha."

The porcelain cat dangled from a branch with a string of painted Christmas lights wrapped around her while balancing on the famous Spode Christmas tree saucer.

I gently lifted it from the branch and spun around to see Maya texting someone before eyeing me.

"Who are you talking to?" I asked.

"Oh, just my sister. She's wondering how it's going at the store." Her eyes avoided mine, and I knew it was all lies.

It was the Sunshine Breakfast Club on the other end

of that phone.

"Do you mind telling Millie that I'll be over to the holiday bazaar with my fudge right after I purchase the cat for Hunter?"

Maya blushed and let out a big sigh. "Are we that obvious?"

"A little." I followed Maya to the cash register and took a sip of cider. "He's coming up for dinner tonight and will be staying around town for a couple of days."

"Oh, really." She rang me up, and I handed her my card.

"Yup." I smiled. "Might as well get everything out in the open."

Maya gave me a grateful smile. "You know, I wouldn't be doing this if I didn't think you and Hunter were a good match."

She wrapped the ornament in white tissue and gently placed it into a paper bag.

"I know. Who do you think was on the other end of the shenanigans for you and Cash?" I winked at Maya and made my way out the door to Foxy. I placed the package inside, and she started right up.

Large snowflakes fell from the sky with the intention of sticking, and I hoped it wouldn't be a tough drive for

Hunter tonight. I turned into the parking lot of the community center and found a parking space near the door. None of the signs were up for the bazaar yet, so I'd made it on time.

I checked my phone just to see if Hunter had responded, and he still hadn't.

Kind of odd.

But nothing to get crazy over.

Right?

I let out a sigh and chuckled to Foxy. "I really need to learn how to handle dating." I turned her off, and she coughed with a crackle so loud I nearly jumped out of my skin. "Foxy, don't you do this to me."

This was not the moment to have her die on me, but I wouldn't worry about it now. Hopefully, she'd start right up when it was time to leave.

In the meantime, I could deliver the fudge and maybe wander around some of the tables in search of the perfect gift for Jackson Jr. and Grace.

A few more cars pulled into the parking lot as I got out of my car and carefully maneuvered the four trays of fudge for the bazaar.

A white blanket of snow covered the ground as an older man sprinkled salt on the walkway.

"Good afternoon, Miss," he said with a twinkle in his

eyes.

I almost didn't recognize Millie's boyfriend, Jackson Sr. "Hey, there. Is Millie inside?"

"She sure is. Go on in."

"See you later," I told Jackson as I made my way down the sidewalk.

Christmas carols piped through the air as I got closer, and an elf opened the door for me to come inside. I glanced around the lobby and saw the double doors open with red, white, and green balloons floating around a life-size gingerbread house and Santa Claus sitting on a throne.

He caught my gaze and winked at me, and I winked back.

Several tables had been covered in baked goods, so I made my way and set my trays down next to a mountain of Christmas sugar cookies before wandering out to find the vendor tables in one of the other rooms.

The scents of pine and chocolate drifted down the hall, and I decided my best bet was to head down the hall until I hit the largest room.

The scene in front of me looked like a living, breathing Christmas card come to life. Twinkling lights covered every post and beam possible. Festive music floated through the air as vendors hurriedly worked to finish decorating their booths.

I unzipped my coat and unwrapped my red scarf, but I kept my knit hat on. A booth with hand-crafted scarves in every color imaginable caught my eye in the corner. An elderly lady whom I didn't recognize sat on a stool, crocheting away, when her eyes caught mine. A red and green scarf pooled next to her as she continued crocheting.

"How are you, dear?"

I nodded with a smile. "I'm doing great, but I'm in awe of your talent. I've never been able to get beyond a simple chain."

She smiled. "It just takes practice and patience."

"And talent," I chimed in as she went back to focusing on her current project.

I scanned the room for Millie, but I hadn't seen her yet. Instead, I found a stall covered in gingerbread ornaments. Each design was ornate and filled with sparkling beads and glitter to make each tiny house, gingerbread person, and animal stand out from one another. Two kids came toddling from that booth and smiled at me before dashing away from the ornaments.

Laughter and murmurs filled the air as I wandered through the holiday bazaar, realizing what a sense of community Buttercup Lake embraced. Neighbors, friends, and family greeted one another with hugs and good cheer while embracing new visitors to our tiny town on the lake.

As I kept walking through the booths, I'd catch snippets of conversations about school plays, family visits, and holiday recipes. It was such a sweet reminder about the connections and traditions weaving themselves through our lives.

I thought about Hunter and the incredible speech he gave that night at the tree-lighting ceremony. And all the money he donated to the Children's Hospital. The thought alone made my heart squeeze with admiration for him. He had a way with words, but the way I felt the moment his eyes connected with mine through the crowd made me feel like I was the only one in his world.

With a smile touching my lips from the memory, I nearly ran over Millie, who'd stepped out in front of me from the hot chocolate stand. Her eyes landed on mine, and she flashed a huge grin.

"Where's the fudge?" she asked, clapping her hands together. "The auction is going live in ten minutes when we open the doors to the public."

"Oh, I put it with the other baked goods down the hall."

Millie frowned. "What other baked goods?"

"Wasn't that room with Santa where I was supposed to put the fudge?"

Millie's arms flew to her slender hips. "What do you mean, Santa?"

"I swear I'm not making things up. Santa is down the hall, an elf opened the door for me, and there were tables of cookies, candies, and everything in between."

Millie turned around with a scowl. "We need to get to the bottom of this."

Without a second lost, Millie marched out of the bazaar with me on her tail when I spotted a long line of kids and their parents coming from the room with Santa.

"See? There." I pointed to the open set of double doors, revealing Santa and all of the sweets.

"That's not part of the bazaar." She shook her head as we headed over to the reader board for the day's events.

Millie pulled out her reading glasses and narrowed her eyes as she scanned the sign. "That's for an auction tonight after Santa."

"Oh, no," I hissed with my eyes wide. "We need that fudge back."

I'd only gotten three hours of sleep because of that fudge. I would not let the Sunshine Breakfast Club down.

I darted toward the room with Millie calling from

behind. "Don't do it. Grace already…" I couldn't hear what she was saying because several kids started making a fuss as I worked my way through the line to get into the room.

When I'd finally made my way to the doors, Santa cocked his head, and I pointed at the sweets table.

He shook his head.

I scowled.

A parent tapped my shoulder, and I dashed to the table where my four trays of fudge sat.

"Miss, what on earth are you doing?" Santa asked as the crowd fell silent.

"It's my fudge."

Santa shook his head. "The fudge is for a good cause."

I grabbed the stack, nodding. "Yes, it is."

"Miss, put the fudge down."

"It's my fudge."

"It's the charity's fudge."

I glanced at the crowd looking at me. "It's meant for the bazaar. I just dropped it off in the wrong room."

Santa shook his head. "I've been here the entire time, and I don't recall you delivering those trays."

I stomped my foot, and the crowd hushed. "You winked at me."

"I don't wink."

Completely exasperated, I shook my head, clutching my fudge. "Look, I'm sure your party is for a good cause, too, but I was up all night making this for the holiday bazaar. I'm exhausted. All eyes are on me. I just want to deliver the fudge to where it belongs, do a little shopping, and go home to make a pot roast for a man who isn't responding to my texts."

Millie walked into the room and came over to help me with the fudge. She glanced at Santa and twirled her finger next to her head before draping her small arms over my shoulders.

"Maybe we should just let them have the fudge," Millie whispered.

"No, it's my fudge until someone buys it, and I will get it to where it needs to go."

Millie tried not to chuckle as the crowd of parents and children parted to let us out of Santa's workshop when I noticed a sign.

Santa's Holiday Workshop
Noon – Five O'clock: Santa Visits
Five O'clock: Mr. Claus's Sweet Auction Benefiting
Elder Care of Wisconsin
Six O'clock: Spaghetti dinner

"Oh, no." I shook my head.

"That's what I was trying to tell you." She shook her head.

I groaned in complete embarrassment. "Great. Hunter spends his life donating money to hospitals, and I spend mine taking it away. At least when Grace stole her food back from a wedding, it was a wedding… not a charity."

"It was only fudge, dear. It's going to be just fine." She took two of the trays from the stack and laughed.

"I think I'm just exhausted and confused." We started walking back to the bazaar.

"Confused? Over what?"

Oh, crud. I stepped right into that one.

"Hunter had sent me a text yesterday that he was going to be up here today, but I haven't heard from him since."

"I'm sure he's just on the road."

"Oh, there's his mom now." Millie elbowed me.

Hunter's mom's gaze skipped over Millie and landed on me, looking like a deer in headlights.

And that was when the pieces of the puzzle started to fit together.

Brielle was back in town, and nobody knew how to tell me it was over between us before it ever began.

Chapter Eighteen

Hunter

I felt overcome with emotion as I held my son. Brielle had left me in her hotel suite with a nanny while she went out to do some shopping.

The moment I found out I had a son, the world faded away. All I wanted was to meet the little man who'd already made the world a better place.

The first ten minutes of finding out that Brielle had our child without telling me brought anger, confusion, loss, and extreme euphoria compacted into one moment of realizing none of that mattered.

What mattered now was that I made sure I was always

there for my son.

Tate.

Tate Knox.

As I held the little guy in my arms, I rocked him asleep while I sat in an uncomfortable hotel room chair and overlooked the city.

His pursed lips, steady breathing, and peach complexion made me wish I hadn't missed so many firsts.

But I had to stay focused on the fact that I had him now.

He felt like a little potato in my arms, swaddled into a warm cocoon.

"He looks so content," Amy said, smiling at me. She was one of Tate's nannies. From what I could gather from Brielle, he had two.

"You think?" I asked, unable to take my eyes off him.

"Absolutely." She hummed to herself as she folded Tate's clothes, and I stayed still, worried I'd disturb him beyond the gentle sway of my body. The sound reminded me of Daisy, and my heart clenched.

How would she take this?

I didn't even know where to start.

Just out of the blue, I'd turned into a father.

Tate's Dad.

I smiled at the thought as I tried to memorize every little thing about him.

The sound of the electronic door lock buzzed through the hotel room, and I looked over to see Brielle coming in with several bags looped around her wrist.

She smiled at me and glanced at Amy, who made herself scarce.

"How'd everything go?" Brielle asked, taking a seat in the chair across from me.

"He's been incredible. Just sleeping in between staring at me. Amy had me feed him, and he drank it all up, did a big burp, followed by a dopey smile, which meant something I didn't understand until Amy cued me in."

Brielle laughed. "Don't ever tell Nick this, but Tate's never been that content in his arms."

I looked at my ex and realized she did have the ability to be kind after all, and I appreciated it more than she knew at this particular moment.

"I'll never tell." I looked back down at my son.

There were so many questions churning through my mind. Brielle and I weren't together. I lived in Wisconsin. She lived in Chicago when she wasn't busy traipsing around the world with her hedge fund fiancé, so how would I get to see my son? Who would decide on the day-to-day tasks? His schooling?

My heart raced with the unknown as Tate stirred in my arms, his little mouth puckering as his blue eyes opened to see mine.

"I'm so relieved." She sighed, stretching her legs.

"Really?"

She nodded. "You're a natural."

"I am in awe, Brielle. We did good."

Her eyes connected with mine, and she nodded. "It's the one good thing that came out of... us."

I chuckled, nodding. "When we go out, we go out with a bang."

She smiled, watching Tate, and brought her eyes back to mine.

"I don't know how else to say this, but I want to be a part of my son's life. A big part."

"Absolutely." She nodded.

"I already missed so much of my little man's life that the thought of missing any more firsts is crippling." And it was true. I didn't understand how, in the span of seconds, I suddenly didn't care about the world spinning around me as the love I felt for my son swelled up inside me.

"Nick and I discussed options, and we have no problem sending Amy up with Tate whenever you'd like to visit him."

Visits with him? I wanted more than that.

"Brielle, I don't just want to visit Tate. I want to help raise him. I don't know what that means or how that looks, but that's what I want."

She was eerily quiet for a few minutes as my pulse pounded. I certainly had done well for myself, but I was no match financially for someone like Nick. If they wanted to drag this through the courts, it would be financially debilitating.

Brielle stood and walked over to the window, looking down at the city. "Nick said this might happen."

"It did."

She turned slowly, bringing her gaze to mine. "It's why I took so long to decide how and when to tell you. Once I found out my son wasn't his, I knew I would tell you. I just needed time to acclimate to all the what-ifs."

I nodded. "I understand."

"And I don't want people to think I'm a terrible mom."

I frowned. "No one would."

She shrugged. "My family already disapproves of me having nannies."

I chuckled, shaking my head. I knew who in particular

would in her family. "So, your mom is willing to watch Tate round the clock?"

Brielle laughed. "So, what are you thinking, Hunter?"

"Shared custody."

Her hand rested on the window. "Every other week?"

"For now, maybe that's the best. I'd like to think we're adult enough to figure things out as they come."

She bit her lip, and I knew she was holding something back. It was going too simply. I could feel it. A bomb was about to be dropped.

"In preparation for this, Nick bought us a small craftsman just down the road from you." She let out a deep breath.

I stared at Brielle. "In Madison?"

She shook her head.

"You hate Buttercup Lake. You despise that they don't have a Starbucks."

"But I love my son more."

She grinned as I tried to formulate exactly what she was telling me.

"Why not a place in Madison?"

"Nick said that a house in Buttercup Lake would be a better investment." She shrugged. "And you always found any excuse to head up there, so I figure you'll move back one day."

I was starting to sweat, and I didn't know if it was because Tate was so warm in my arms or because my ex was about to move a few doors down from me.

"I have been spending more time in Buttercup Lake." I nodded slowly, trying to formulate what my life was about to look like.

I looked down at Tate and around the hotel suite. My life had become...

Surreal.

That was the only term I could think of that aptly described the state of my world.

This morning, I'd been daydreaming about how to convince Daisy to become my girlfriend, and now I sat here with my ex, holding a treasure I couldn't even fully comprehend yet.

Whenever I looked at Brielle, there was an air of awkwardness between us, a mutual understanding that we were through.

We were done.

But now, we were forever connected.

Nothing would change that, and we needed to fully come around to the idea.

Holding Tate in my arms made it abundantly clear

that nothing mattered between Brielle and me any longer.

"So, where did we go wrong?" Brielle teased.

"I think the list would be shorter if we started at when were they right?"

She snorted and shook her head. "Remember when we went on that camping trip with your brother?"

"Oh, the stories I'll be able to tell Tate about his 6-inch-heel-wearing mother in the backcountry of Wisconsin."

"You wouldn't." She narrowed her eyes on me.

"I don't know. Your falling into the shrubs was pretty…"

Brielle laughed, shaking her head. "It's too bad our time together wasn't spent like this."

I shook my head. "No, things worked out how they were supposed to."

She nodded. "They really did."

"How about that time you were supposed to be reading me the directions from my phone on the road trip to the Crystal Caves?"

Brielle groaned. "Why would you ever think I wanted to go to them in the first place?"

I chuckled, knowing Daisy would. "And before we knew it, we took the wrong county road and wound up face-to-face in a field with a cow."

213

She let out a deep breath and nodded. "A very angry cow."

I grinned, looking down at Tate, who stirred and wiggled his nose. "But all of that led us to this, and I wouldn't take back a second."

"All those fights." She shook her head. "We're just not meant for one another."

"No, we're not, but this little guy will be dynamite with our DNA in him."

She snickered. "Indeed."

I looked at the mother of my son and realized how we were never meant to be. But this banter, we could do. Getting deep wasn't our strong suit.

But with Daisy, I craved the layers and the intensity of our discussions. Daisy was everything I needed and more. My only hope was that this wouldn't be too much, too soon.

And if it were, I'd understand.

This would be a lot for anyone.

If I weren't holding Tate in my arms this very second, I wouldn't be inclined to believe it, either.

"What are your plans for December?" I asked Brielle.

"Well, skiing is out. Nick just screwed up his knee playing tennis. Plus, his mom's health isn't great. I think we plan on staying home in Chicago."

I nodded, not believing what I was about to ask.

But I had to. The thought of being separated from Tate any longer made every part of my body tense.

"What about coming up to Buttercup Lake for the holiday?" I cleared my throat. "Maybe we could hammer out more of the custody details."

She didn't look sold on the idea.

"Come on, small-town life isn't a disease. Our local coffee shop is way better than your current addiction."

"I'll think about it and talk it over with Nick."

I nodded, hating that my future time spent with my son was dependent on others playing nicely.

And then it dawned on me.

"Wait a second. Are you moving into that remodeled craftsman on the lake?"

She nodded. "Yeah. That's the one. We signed the papers two weeks ago."

"Wow. I never would have expected that in my wildest dreams."

Brielle laughed and shook ahead. "Go on. Go ahead and say it."

"Say what?"

"Or your worst nightmares."

I chuckled, shaking my head as I tried to imagine how

Daisy would react to her new neighbor.

Chapter Nineteen

Daisy

I stared at the empty platter that once held two pounds of pot roast. I messaged Hunter before I put the roast in, wanting to confess my embarrassing Santa moment and find out when he thought he might make it to Buttercup Lake.

It wasn't until the roast dinged in the oven that he messaged that he wouldn't be coming up just yet. The cryptic tone in the text worried me. I suddenly felt a distance between us, but I didn't know if that was in my head because I knew Brielle came to see him or if he'd gone back to being the aloof Hunter I'd first met.

The thought put a burning pit in my stomach, but not

for long.

The moment I took out the tender roast and placed it on the carving board, it nearly shredded and cut itself.

Hunter was really missing out, and by the time I'd knocked at least half the meat back, a few potatoes, some carrots, and celery, I realized I was eating my emotions.

But I didn't care. A nagging feeling pressed its way into me, and I ate a little more until I was miserable and finally put about a quarter of the roast away.

No one ever needed to know that I ate a pound and a half or more of beef.

But honestly.

Who did Brielle think she was, and if Hunter couldn't just tell her to leave him alone, then that told me a lot about Hunter.

I also realized that I wasn't one of those people who could just sleep with someone without getting... attached. I liked Hunter a lot. But maybe I didn't see clearly enough, or I jumped in too soon. He'd obviously demonstrated a pattern with Brielle.

For the first time, it felt like the Sunshine Breakfast Club had lost their way. I shoved myself back from the table and groaned my agony into the palms of my hands. I didn't know which hurt worse, my stomach or thinking that Hunter got swayed by Brielle again.

The thought tore me up inside.

I'd finally let myself open up to a person, and he was emotionally unavailable.

How ironic.

And then the look Hunter's mom flashed me at the holiday bazaar. It was a cross between pity and...

No, it's just pity.

Or was it concern?

My doorbell rang, and a ridiculous amount of hope filled my veins, thinking it was Hunter.

But when I got to the door and opened it, I saw Maya, Nina, Grace, Millie, and even Abby from the coffee shop standing on my stoop. Their expressions were void of any emotion.

This couldn't be good.

They charged right into the house and beelined for the living room.

"Welcome," I said with a laugh.

Millie took a seat on the couch. "I wanted to get my book back."

I shook my head, bewildered. "Your book?"

"The one for the book club. I decided we were switching gears. We're reading *A Christmas Carol* after all."

I chuckled, thinking she was kidding, but she was very serious.

"Does this have to do with my Santa run-in?" I asked.

"The book," Millie repeated, holding out her hand.

All the women stared at me, and I realized they weren't going to leave unless I handed it over, and I was exhausted.

They couldn't stay.

I chuckled and shook my head. "Okay, okay. It's in my bedroom. I'll go get it."

As I trundled to my bedroom, I wondered what had gotten into these ladies. It was just a book.

I scanned my nightstand and didn't see it, but when I turned around, I saw it propped on the pine dresser next to my naughty Christmas gnome.

I took the bookmark out of this Christmas love story, knowing I'd just buy myself a copy, and wandered back into my living room to see everyone had made themselves comfortable.

"How are you doing, Daisy?" Maya asked.

I looked at each woman staring at me before turning my attention to Millie. "What's going on?"

"We don't know," Millie said with a shrug.

"Okay. I'm not sure what you're talking about, and

I'm really not sure what I'm talking about. Did you want some coffee or wine?"

Abby nodded. "I wouldn't mind some wine."

Nina elbowed her, and she shrugged. "What? I'm thirsty."

I chuckled. "Red or white?"

"White." She grinned as Millie followed me into the kitchen. Since it was an open floor plan, I wasn't sure why she felt the need to be suddenly close.

Reaching for a glass, I felt Millie inch up on me. "Is everything okay, Millie? Do you need some wine?"

I set the glass on the counter, grabbed an unopened bottle from the fridge, and poured some for Nina.

"No, I'm fine. It makes me get up and pee all night."

I laughed, walking over to Nina with the glass. "I've never heard of that."

"You just wait." Millie waggled her finger. "Once you hit eighty, everything makes you pee."

"I'll have to remember that tip."

I looked at the top members of the infamous book club and raised my brows. "So, how are things?" I bounced my gaze from Millie to Maya, to Grace, to Nina, and to Abby.

Millie sat on the couch next to Nina. "I want to apologize."

"That came out of nowhere," I said, shaking my head.

"I think over the years, I've gotten cocky, Daisy. I see matches. I pick books. I manipulate circumstances. I have helpers all over Wisconsin…" She bit her lip and stared at my Christmas tree. "We've had a near-perfect record."

I nodded. "It's been fun. I don't think I could have had a better welcome to Buttercup Lake than working on Grace's hookup."

Grace smiled. "And for that, I'm forever grateful."

Millie scowled. "But it was bound to happen."

"What was?"

"Hunter's not the one for you."

I chuckled and shook my head. "That's not quite how I see it."

Millie's expression remained stoic. "It's true."

I tipped my head. "Are you just playing off my stubborn side? Like if you tell me he's not good for me, you'll know I'll go running to him?"

She chuckled and shook her head. "No, that's a good angle to use, but I actually mean it."

The tension in the room was building, and I couldn't for the life of me figure out what was going on.

"Well, this is a bit of a pickle because…" I looked at all the ladies. "I really like him. We're really connecting. In fact, I think he's coming up here tomorrow."

Millie shook her head. "I'm not sure he is, Daisy."

I frowned and shook my head.

"Wait. What do you mean?"

I didn't want to hear the name.

"I'm all about honesty." Millie let out a disgruntled sigh.

"That's comforting." I nodded. "I am, too."

Nobody said anything for a few seconds, and I finally couldn't handle it any longer.

"Is it Brielle? He was meeting with her one last time at his bar. Is that it?" I looked at Maya and then at Millie. "Are they back together?"

Saying the words seemed surreal.

"We know Hunter is a little… immature," Millie started. "But after this last year, I thought maybe he'd outgrown some of that."

I shook my head. "He's not immature. He's responsible and caring."

Millie put her hands in her lap. "I don't want to be the one to have to tell you this, but my friend's daughter saw Hunter walking into a hotel down in Madison with Brielle."

It felt like the room leaned to the left, or maybe it was the Christmas tree that leaned.

Or was it me?

"Impossible." I thought back to the words he told me when we'd slept together. None of it added up.

She shook her head. "I'm sorry. I just wanted to be upfront about it. Maya mentioned that you were onto us, and I thought the best way to go about this problem was to be frank."

I nodded, realizing it wasn't the room or the tree leaning. It was me, leaning against Nina. She pulled me close.

"Hunter's a good guy. He just might have made a mistake," Nina whispered.

Millie scowled. "That's not a mistake. You don't just accidentally roll out of a taxicab and into someone's hotel room by mistake. That takes thought, determination, and... it's just plain mean."

But I knew Hunter was none of those things, and I was shocked his two sisters-in-law weren't trying to get to the bottom of things.

"Cash can't believe it. He's so pissed at Hunter right now."

I thought back to the funny look on Hunter's mom at the bazaar. "Does his mom know?"

Millie grunted. "I'm beginning to think so because she's been stone-cold silent. Not a peep out of her. No message was returned. Nothing. In fact, she barely spent any time at the bazaar."

I sat up and let out a groan as I let my head fall into my hands. This was what breaking down my walls got me, but I couldn't wait to let Hunter have it.

Maybe disconnect his heated seats when he's least expecting it... possibly right before he's about to pick up the other woman.

Hmph.

Hunter's eyes flashed through my mind right before we kissed goodbye the other day. Warmth spread through me, and I shook my head.

"Nope. I don't believe it. He's not back with Brielle." I grabbed the book out of Millie's hands. "The book is back on."

"No, it's not." Millie shook her head, grabbing it back.

I chuckled. "Yes, it is. We're supposed to have chapters nine through seventeen read by Tuesday, and we had better all show up ready to discuss. And I'll even have a report for you guys about... things."

"Daisy, I rarely put my foot down, but I must. The evidence isn't looking good." She shook her head. "And I don't want you and Hunter... I don't want Hunter to sweet-talk you into engaging in a special waltz. You know, step into the ring before you're ready. Or bake a cake without all the ingredients, if you know what I mean."

I nervously laughed, trying to shove away the worry swelling through me about Hunter and Brielle. "I have no idea what you're talking about."

"Listen, I don't want you to let Hunter plant his seed in the garden because he knows how to swoon the pants off you." She stared at me, her eyes widening. "Oh, no. You two already…"

My cheeks flushed with embarrassment.

"That was the euphemistic tour de force of avoiding the sex talk if I've ever heard one." Grace grimaced.

Millie shook her head. "That's why you're not thinking straight. You already let the tadpole into the pond. Don't worry. I know how it goes. I jumped into the sheets with Jackson Sr. on date two, but that turned out just fine."

Maya winced, hearing the news from her grandma, as I stifled a laugh and brought my gaze back to Millie's.

"I believe in Hunter, and I'll wait for his explanation." I smiled, shaking my head. "And it had better be one hell of a good one."

Millie straightened, looking extremely regal as she handed the book back to me. "You're a better woman than I,

Daisy."

I smiled, shaking my head. "I'm just running on hope."

Chapter Twenty

Hunter

I looked down at the text from Daisy, and I knew I needed to talk with her.

Rumors are flying around town, and I'm trying not to believe a single one.

I bit my lip as I studied the upside-down emoji sent at the end of the text. I think that meant she wasn't worried about whatever she heard.

But I didn't know what she'd heard. The only person in Buttercup Lake who knew about my son was my mom. I didn't even let her tell my dad because out of the two, he had a bigger mouth.

And this wasn't something I wanted to get back to Daisy without telling her first.

But why would there be any rumors flying if my mom didn't say anything? I reached for my phone and texted her.

Have you told anyone about Tate?

She responded almost immediately.

Not a soul

I wrote back a thank you, put my phone on the counter, and walked over to the tree. Daisy's photo dangling from the branch brought a smile to my lips. I missed her so much.

I had to tell her what was going on. She more than deserved to know, but it wasn't like I could just take a selfie with Tate and me and send it on over.

I needed to tell her in person, explain the complexities and the confusion and everything in between, but I couldn't just yet.

Nick was flying in today on his private jet and would

be coming over with Brielle and Tate in the next hour sometime. The whole situation seemed like I was on the outside looking in.

There were so many emotions swirling around inside that I didn't even know what to say to Daisy yet. I wouldn't say I was in disbelief, but I kind of was. Not to mention, I was attempting to work through the anger and annoyance of just finding out about having a son.

I had to remind myself that I was lucky to find out at all. Brielle could have chosen not to tell me.

My phone buzzed, and I walked over to my cell to see another text from Daisy.

I don't know what's going on, but I know something is. I am here for you, no matter what or how you need it.

My heart raced when I realized she was second-guessing our relationship. She was preparing to put herself back in the friend zone.

I shook my head as I quickly typed a text back.

I hope to be up there tonight. I'll explain more when I get there, but I can't even begin to figure out a way to tell you everything that has happened in my life in the last twenty-

four hours. Don't believe the rumors, whatever they are.

I hit *Send*, and the doorbell chimed. For some reason, I felt nervous. I couldn't wait to see Tate again, but it felt extremely strange to be inviting my ex and her fiancé into my place, knowing he'd originally thought the baby was his.

I reached the door and swung it open to see Brielle, Nick, Amy, and Tate in a buggy.

Nick's eyes connected with mine, and I extended my hand for a sturdy handshake before inviting everyone in.

"Nice to meet you, Nick."

"Likewise."

"Come on in."

Brielle glided in like she owned the place, and Nick followed closely behind. His dark suit fit snugly on his slender flame. Amy wheeled the buggy in, and I couldn't help but peer in to see Tate. His eyes were wide as he took in his surroundings.

"He is a handsome fellow," Nick said.

"I am in awe," I confessed.

Nick nodded. "The moment I found out that I wasn't the father, I knew we had to get in touch."

"I know this isn't the most traditional of circumstances, so I appreciate it."

Brielle wandered to the tree as I stared at Tate.

Amy smiled at me. "Did you want to hold him? He just woke up."

I nodded. "I'd love to. I need to get as much of this in as possible."

Amy unbuckled him and lifted him out of the buggy. He was dressed in a dapper green sweater and black corduroys. I could picture him playing rugby in a blink of an eye.

His warm body snuggled right into me, and I let out a slow, relaxed breath.

"Who's this?" Brielle asked, pointing at a picture of Daisy. "I feel like I've seen her before."

I nodded. "She lives in Buttercup Lake and was at some of the festivities you attended with me."

She snickered. "If that's what you want to call them."

Nick glanced at me apologetically, but I was accustomed to Brielle's love affair with where I grew up. I honestly didn't know how she was going to manage coming up to visit when I had Tate. She hated the place.

One step at a time.

"Are you dating?" She eyed me with lifted brows. Now, it was my turn to look at Nick apologetically.

"Yeah. I just started seeing her."

She snapped her fingers. "Wait a minute. She's that woman you hired last year, slobbering all over you."

I laughed, rocking Tate slowly. "I don't quite remember it that way."

Brielle didn't continue, but I walked over to the couch while she stood staring at the photo.

"Can I get you three anything?" I asked.

Brielle held up her Starbucks cup while Nick shook his head. I glanced over at Amy, who looked like she'd love something.

"Did you want water, soda, anything?"

"I'd love water." Amy smiled. "But let me get it. Just point me to the right cabinet."

Brielle dragged her gaze from the photo to the tree and sighed. "I'll get it for you."

Nick took a seat in one of the wing chairs across from Tate and me.

"I wanted to talk in person, get a feel for your expectations, schedules, things like that." Nick leaned forward.

"Clearly, I want to be involved in my son's life as much as possible." My pulse quickened. "Brielle mentioned you bought a place."

"We did, and there's a small airport there in town that

we can fly into."

Oh, right. Private.

"Our lives aren't very predictable, and we do a lot of traveling. It has slowed down some, but I expect things to pick back up."

"Tate is always welcome to stay with me."

Nick nodded. "I got that impression from Brielle. I'm not a fool. I know there's going to be some rough patches and misunderstandings, but I truly believe there is nothing better for Tate than having you in his life as much as possible."

"I appreciate that. I imagine it could have taken a different turn."

Nick shook his head. "I grew up with a distant father, and I wouldn't wish that on my worst enemy."

"I propose that Tate will fly in on the first of every month and will be picked up on the fifteenth to come back to Chicago." He glanced at Brielle, who was coming over to sit.

She looked at me. "It's less back and forth that way."

"If you, for any reason, need to be in Chicago for Tate, we will send the plane."

I smiled. "Very kind of you, but the drive isn't that bad."

"If that sounds acceptable, I can have my lawyers draw up some documents that you can have reviewed, and we can go from there."

Tate started to stir as if he could sense my panic about their impending departure.

"That sounds like a fantastic plan." I looked at Brielle. "When can I expect to see Tate again?"

"We thought we'd fly into Buttercup Lake a little over a week from now so we can check out the new place. I already hired a designer, so furniture should be arriving shortly."

"Wow. Okay." The thought of being without Tate for that long was rough, but it had to be done. "That's great. I know his grandparents will be thrilled to meet him."

Brielle's expression softened. "He's going to have a very interesting upbringing."

I sat him on my knee, and I swore he smiled, which made Amy laugh since we both knew what that meant.

Amy walked over and picked up Tate.

"I don't mind helping," I told her.

She nodded and motioned for me to lead the way to a good changing spot.

And that was the first moment I realized I had absolutely nothing in the way of baby needs. Suddenly, it felt like I was a complete wreck. I'd need diapers, a changing table, a crib, and baby gates for when he started crawling. I needed toys, clothes...

A cold sweat trickled down my back as I thought about how truly unprepared I was.

I motioned for Amy to follow me into a small study where I had an oversized plush ottoman to lay him on. She whipped a diaper and baby wipes out of nowhere.

"Nearly all of his outfits have snaps. See?"

She raised the little guy's legs, and sure enough, all along the inner seams were snaps. She did a quick un-Velcro of his diaper with his legs up while sliding in the new diaper. All the while, with the extra tentacles she suddenly grew, she'd managed to wipe his rear with a baby wipe while rolling up the dirty diaper.

"See? Simple as that."

I chuckled, looking at Tate's little legs as she snapped him back up.

"You look terrified," she said, smiling at me.

"Honestly, I don't want to screw him up."

She shook her head. "You're here, aren't you?" She glanced around the quiet study. "That's half the battle. Besides, it sounds like I'll be coming with Tate every time he comes here or to Buttercup Lake."

"Oh, wow. Okay."

She picked him up and handed him to me. "Do you have a place for this?"

I nodded, took the diaper from her, and tossed it in the garbage can next to my desk.

She grinned and nodded. "Whatever you do, don't forget you put it there."

I laughed, holding up Tate as he cooed. "That sounds like one of the most important things someone has told me."

She nodded. "It is. Believe me."

As we made our way into the living room, Nick and Brielle were looking at the lake.

"First diaper lesson down," Amy said.

Brielle turned around. "That's the easy part. Just wait until two o'clock in the morning comes."

"What happens at two?"

"Nick likes to call it 'the witching hour'."

I chuckled as Nick looked at his phone. "I hate to do this, but our flight is in an hour. I have a meeting I have to get back in town for."

My chest tightened at the thought of giving Tate back, but I knew this was the new normal. Soon, I'd get to spend days and weeks with him, even if Brielle was lurking somewhere.

Brielle looked over and gave me a sympathetic smile. Motherhood had somehow softened her, and I was extremely grateful.

"We can do some video calls this week and go over the paperwork for custody." Brielle tilted her head with sympathy.

It felt like my world was slowly imploding. The elation and jubilation soaring through my veins over meeting my son, to the heartache and disbelief that I wouldn't get to see him for days, felt like a nightmare rollercoaster. The stark reminder lingered as I nosed him with mine and gave his little body another embrace as Amy came over to bundle him up for the cold weather.

"I can't wait," I said, watching Tate get buckled into his buggy.

Brielle drew a breath and glanced at Nick. "There's one more thing I wanted to talk to you about."

"Okay." My eyes stayed on hers.

"Nick and I are getting married the day after Christmas."

I smiled and nodded. "Congratulations."

"Thanks." She grinned and looked at Nick. "But we wanted to head to Bora Bora for our honeymoon."

My heart sank.

More time to be away from Tate.

"And I don't think I should bring Tate." Her brows rose. "Amy would be with you, and we'd make sure you had anything you needed."

"Wow. That's incredible. I'm beyond excited."

"It's for three weeks."

I smiled, glancing at my little buddy. "Even better. I'm up for it. I'll take time off from the bar, and I'll stay in Buttercup Lake near family."

Relief flooded through Brielle. "Thank you so much. The thought of trying to enjoy my honeymoon while balancing motherhood and…" She stopped. "No, that sounds awful. It came out wrong."

One thing I knew was that Brielle always told me she didn't want children, but I was completely in awe at the ease and grace with which she mothered Tate. The children issue was always a deal breaker for us. I smiled at the irony as Brielle walked over to Tate and bent over to kiss him before Amy strolled out the door with him.

"No, I understand." I nodded, glancing at Nick, who looked adoringly at Brielle.

But I desperately wanted to give Tate another taste of life where nannies didn't take care of his every whim.

"I can't wait to get to know my son," I told them. "So, please feel free to honeymoon for as long as you want."

Brielle laughed. "You might be singing a different tune when you're running on no sleep."

I grinned and nodded, knowing I'd be counting the seconds for that opportunity, but now, it was my time to figure out how to tell Daisy.

Chapter Twenty-One

Daisy

The coffee shop was a riot of Christmas cheer, but the festive mood felt like a stark contrast to the chaos thrashing inside my heart. My chest ached with confusion from Hunter's random texts. But I believed more than anything that he wasn't back with Brielle.

Most likely.

I groaned and put my head in my palms as Abby laughed behind me.

"I hope this drink cheers you up," she teased, rubbing my back. She bent over and brought her mouth to my ear. "I put a little Schnapps in it. Shh. Don't tell anyone."

I sat up and chuckled. "It's eleven in the morning."

"And not a second too soon." She winked at me and wandered back to behind the counter as a line formed through the café.

I looked around, and comfort wrapped itself around me. I needed to be in the mix of Buttercup Lake, to feel the festive mood, the celebratory dance of the holidays, and try to drown out my own thoughts.

I sipped my peppermint mocha, the warmth barely registering, but the Schnapps certainly did. Abby's gaze met mine, and she waggled her brows. I shook my head teasingly before sitting back in my chair to try to ignore the nagging pit in my stomach.

Red, silver, and green garlands twisted around the wooden beams. A tiny Christmas tree had been placed on each table, twinkling with miniature multicolored lights.

A large tree stood in the corner with shimmering gold and silver ornaments as the warm glow of the overhead lights sprinkled down. But as I sat and watched smiling faces, listened to the chatter, and heard the holiday music through the speakers, I realized that all of the Christmas magic in the universe wouldn't lift the weight of worry off my chest.

Not until I saw Hunter and could look into his eyes.

My train of thought was interrupted by the jingle of

bells as an overly enthusiastic elf with cheeks rosy from more than just the cold made his rounds from table to table. He carried bells in one hand and a basket of candy canes in the other while collecting donations for our foodbank.

The elf was a bit too tall for the costume, his green pants comically short while revealing striped purple and white socks that clashed terribly with the rest of his red and green outfit. Green face paint obscured his features, and the elf hat tugged down around his ears made me smile. I hadn't the foggiest who they'd put up to playing the elf.

The elf caught my gaze and winked. "Cheer up, it's Christmas! Remember, Santa's always got his eye on you."

I chuckled. "I'll try to remember that."

He handed me a candy cane, and I stuffed a five-dollar bill in his pouch hooked to his belt.

I thought that meant he'd be on his way, but he took a seat across from me at my table.

"My dogs are tired." He shook his head and stretched out his legs. "This duty is killer. I'd much rather be sitting in my squad car."

I sat up straight. "Wait. Nate?"

He laughed and nodded, bringing his eyes to mine. "Shh. Don't tell anyone. I don't need to show up to a crime scene looking like I butchered an elf."

Sure enough, it was our friendly sheriff.

"Honestly, the things I do for charity."

I smiled and nodded. "At least you didn't steal fudge away from the elderly in need."

His chin raised up in laughter. "I heard about that." His elf hat fell to the floor, and the tinge of green face paint had spread into his hair.

"Seriously?"

"Indeed, I did."

"Well, Nate. You do a lot of good stuff for our community."

He shrugged. "I try. I figure I was such a little jerk as a kid, I'd better make up for it somehow."

"You weren't a jerk, from what I heard, just... mischievous."

A sly grin spread on his lips. "Maybe so. Hey, I heard about Hunter and Brielle. Don't lose sleep over that guy."

My heart clenched. What exactly had he heard?

Abby brought over a fluffy latte for the elf, and I got a whiff of more Schnapps. He flashed me a wicked grin. "It's the only way I can get through four more hours of this, and she promised her husband would drive me home."

I raised my mug and winked. "Hey, I hear you. He'll be giving me a ride, too, if I have another one." I shrugged.

"Although, I'll probably stay here all day so I can keep my mind busy."

"That bad, huh?" He took a sip, his gaze on me over the cup. "I really thought you two had something going. That night of the fire, he looked like he wanted to jump into the building himself if you were inside."

I scowled and nodded. "I know. I thought that, too."

He shook his head and sighed. "It's why I stay single, honestly. It's too much work, and after a hard day of chasing criminals, I just don't have the energy."

I stared at Nate. "Uh, Nate. We don't really seem to have many of those around Buttercup Lake."

He scowled. "Just go with me on this one."

I laughed and shook my head. "Love is a lot of work."

"Actually, finding love is a lot of work. Keeping it? I don't know. I thought that was the hard part," I confessed.

Nate took another sip of his latte. "I don't know. The whole thing just baffles me."

"You're a good-looking guy, Nate. I'm sure once you make up your mind, you'll find someone."

"There is something about you that always brightens my day, Daisy." He shook his head. "Even when you're having a crummy day, you just know how to make people feel better." He tapped his finger on the table. "Hunter is really missing out, and I just might need to remind him of that somehow."

An evil laugh escaped my lips, and I shook my head. "I still have faith. I refuse to believe the rumors."

But I knew that wasn't entirely true, or I wouldn't be sulking in the middle of the coffee shop in Buttercup Lake to try to make myself feel human again.

Nate polished off his latte and held up his candy canes. "Duty calls."

"Have fun with your bells."

He winked at me and rang his bells with enough enthusiasm to wake the dead as he circulated through the coffee shop again.

I couldn't help but think about the absurdity of this holiday season, all because I'd decided to let myself be open and tear down my walls a bit. So, here I was, moping in a coffee shop while a grown man in an elf costume spread questionable cheer, all while still being responsible for the safety of Buttercup Lake. The situation would have been hilarious if it weren't so pathetic.

Glancing around the café, I spotted couples holding hands over their lattes and friends laughing together while little ones ran around the tables.

Was everyone else really as happy as they seemed, or

were they just better at hiding their worries?

With a sigh, I stirred my coffee and Schnapps, watching the whipped cream swirl into the dark liquid. The holidays were supposed to be filled with joy and togetherness, but I felt uncertainty and indigestion from eating my emotions. I knew I needed to talk to Hunter, but the uncertainty and fear almost paralyzed me.

The bells jingled swiftly with a crash, and I looked over to see the elf tripping over a chair, toppling over onto a table. The ridiculousness of the moment broke through my melancholy, and I found myself laughing as Nate stood up and glanced over at me, giving me the booze sign with his hand.

Maybe there was still a little bit of holiday spirit left in me after all.

I finished my peppermint mocha, and Abby brought me another one, but this one without the Schnapps, which was perfect so I could read the next few chapters of our book club selection.

Maybe Millie had been right.

I pulled out the paperback from my purse, the cover featuring a small-town bar with snow speckled on the cover and a windswept heroine in the arms of a dashing yet brooding hero. The sign on the bar was crooked as the title splashed across it.

Settling into my chair, I flipped the page open to chapter nine. Mary was caught in a complicated love affair with a man whom she thought she wanted, but then the man she'd left was truly who she needed. Her heart was torn between wants and needs, and her overall directness zapped me in my place. As I continued flipping the pages and delved deeper into the story, I couldn't escape the chill of recognition that swept through me. Only I wasn't her. She was Hunter.

I groaned and kept my eyes glued to the pages. "Great. Our relationship is a walking cliché."

As I turned the page, the scene in the book shifted away to an over-the-top Christmas party at the bar where Mary found herself stuck in a nightmare with her hero playing Santa and his elves handing out presents. One of the elves was overly enthusiastic, shouting out, "Yule be sorry if you don't try the eggnog." And I couldn't help but picture Nate as the elf and Hunter on the pages I was devouring.

And then it turned quickly. Nate, I mean, the book elf, was the one Mary was torn over, and Santa begged for her to realize he was the one. The next thing I knew, Mary was running out of the bar, screaming. Things were going haywire left and right, and my mind became muddled as I closed the book.

"Whew," I muttered. "Too much for one day."

Maybe, like Mary, I needed to stop overthinking. I'd always been one to take action. I polished off my mocha, the last zip of peppermint mocha stinging my lips, and made a decision. If Hunter wasn't going to come up here and tell me, I was going to go down to Madison.

I was going to get my own happy ending whether I wanted it or not.

Darn it.

I shoved the book back into my purse and shot up from the chair just as I heard the most magical words by an unlikely source.

"Daisy, I heard you were here." His gaze locked on mine, and all my fizzle fizzed as I slumped back into the chair, trying to get a glimpse of my future.

But would it be with or without Hunter?

Chapter Twenty-Two

Hunter

I parked my car with a sense of urgency as my heart pounded against my ribcage. I'd been looking for Daisy since I arrived in Buttercup Lake. I went to her house and didn't see Foxy.

And I couldn't believe that Foxy actually popped into my head when the driveway was empty, but that was Daisy. She had this magical way of enlightening your views on life. A car wasn't just a car. It had personality and a vibe all its own.

I shook my head at the thought of getting to see Daisy

again. I missed her so much it hurt, but I couldn't tell her why I'd stayed in Madison longer. She deserved to hear the truth from my lips, in person.

The weight of my revelation grew heavier with each passing second, and I was relieved to find out from my mom that Maya had noticed Foxy parked down the street from the coffee shop, and Abby confirmed it and had been instructed to keep her here.

That was precisely how the Sunshine Breakfast Club's network functioned. There were literally eyes and ears everywhere, but that also led to trouble at times.

Like now, I didn't know what rumors were swirling around town about me, but I was certain they weren't accurate.

As I pushed open the door, the comforting scents of coffee and cinnamon filled my senses. It was a stark contrast to the chaos stirring inside me.

Christmas cheer in every form adorned Abby's coffee shop, from the Christmas carols softly churning through the speakers to the sparkling garlands wrapped around all the beams, but all I could focus on was Daisy.

Sitting alone at a table, lost in a book.

Daisy looked beautiful as always, but there was a tightness around her eyes, a telltale sign of her worry. My heart ached, knowing I was the root of it.

A faint smile touched her lips, and she shook her head as if to disagree with whatever she'd just read. She leaned back and smiled, taking a sip of her drink before muttering to herself.

She closed the book and shot up from her seat.

I hesitated for a split second, gathering my thoughts. How would I tell the love of my life that my world just got turned upside down? That I had a son I never knew existed with a woman I'd tried to get away from? The weight of this secret that I'd been carrying since I found out felt like a two-ton boulder sinking me into the floor.

But I had to do it. I had to tell her.

"Daisy, I heard you were here," I said.

Her gaze snapped to mine, and I caught my breath at the stunning look in her gaze. Our eyes connected, and I felt that magnetic pull to her that I'd craved. I slowly approached her table.

"Hey." Her voice was barely above a whisper as she sat back down. "I was about to drive to Madison."

My brows shot up in surprise as she motioned for me to take a seat. "You were?"

She laughed softly and nodded. "It turns out I'm not very patient."

"No way…" I teased, feeling the lightness between us that had always been so refreshing. "Listen, I'm so sorry for missing dinner. I'd heard you'd made me an amazing roast."

Embarrassment ticked through her gaze as her smile grew. Daisy leaned over the table slightly. "I ate the whole thing in two days. Most of it, the first night." In a hushed voice, she continued. "I also learned that I eat my emotions." She straightened in her chair but didn't take her eyes away from mine.

"I'm so sorry, Daisy. My world has been turned upside down and right side up again, and everything I thought I knew about my future has been blown out of the water."

She narrowed her eyes on me in a state of nervousness, and my stomach twisted. "Are you back with Brielle?"

"No, nothing like that."

"I'm not going to beat around the bush. I heard you went into a hotel with Brielle."

I nodded. "That's true."

Horror dashed through her gaze, and I reached for her hand. "But not because of that." I took a deep breath, searching for the right words.

"Please just tell me whatever it is you have to say." She glanced around the coffee shop. "It doesn't matter if people hear because they'll somehow know by tomorrow anyhow."

I laughed tenderly, keeping her hands in mine. "I don't know where to start."

"From the beginning," she said simply.

Sympathy wove through her gaze. "But will I need more Schnapps for this?"

I laughed, letting out a deep breath. "Daisy, you might. I'm still in shock myself."

She nodded. "I'll wait to find out what it is before I have any more."

"There's something I found out recently, something big, and it's going to change… everything." I shook my head, feeling her hand squeeze mine. "I can't pretend it won't, and I'll understand if it's just too much."

Her brow furrowed in concern. "What is it? I have to be honest that you're freaking me out."

I took another deep breath. "I have a son."

I'd meant to soften it somehow, but all I could do was blurt it out.

"His name is Tate." The words hung in the air between us, heavy and clouded.

Daisy didn't pull her hand back. Instead, she put her other on top of ours. She cocked her head slightly before shaking it. Confusion darted through her gaze.

"A son?" Daisy's voice was a mix of surprise and bewilderment. "How? When?" And then she laughed. "Wait. Scratch that. I know how. I don't want details."

She pretended to shiver, and I was completely shocked by her response. It was the same old Daisy, confronting news head-on and with a lightness that I craved.

"He's adorable. He looks just like me," I confessed.

Her lip turned up at the corner. "Well, you are adorable."

I smiled, taking in the tenderness of this moment. I didn't know what tomorrow would bring, but in this instant, Daisy didn't run screaming from the coffee shop.

"How old is he?" she asked as Abby brought over my favorite drink, an iced coffee.

"He's five months old."

Daisy's eyes widened. "Wait. He's that old? She just now told you?"

I nodded, relieved that she felt as incensed as I did. "I think she thought or hoped it was Nick's since she was obviously having relationships with both of us."

Daisy whistled.

I laughed, shaking my head. "It's crazy, actually. When you look at Tate, it's like looking at my twin, and he really is the complete opposite of Nick."

Daisy looked intrigued. "How so?"

"Nick has red hair, a fair complexion, very slender." I smiled, thinking about my son. "And Tate is all bulk. He is a thick little guy, and he has blue eyes and my nose."

She chuckled. "And he carries your rugged handsomeness? Sturdy jawline and chiseled features?"

I smiled, loving every second of sharing this information with Daisy. "Yeah, I guess you could see that underneath all the baby chub."

She moved her hands from mine, and I instantly missed her touch. "I can't wait to meet him, but I need more details."

"Well, Nick and Brielle came to Madison on their private jet."

"Wait? What?"

I nodded. "He's a hedge fund guy. Brielle is extremely delighted. Anyway, she came to the bar and told me. And then let me see Tate at her hotel. They have nannies, plural. But Amy seems to be the nanny who travels with Tate the most."

"Oh, wow." Daisy looked impressed.

"And Nick, Brielle, Tate, and Amy all came over to my apartment. We've been loosely talking about how custody will work."

She nodded slowly. "And how will it work?"

"They seem very open to shared custody, and it's a big relief." I smiled, noticing an elf outside jangling bells at people. "I do great with the bar, but if they'd wanted a custody battle, yikes. I don't have unlimited resources like that. But, like I said… Nick seems like a very understanding man."

"I'd imagine." Daisy looked at me in disbelief. "I can't believe you're a dad, but I promise I won't call you Daddy."

"Well, you could…"

"Then maybe I will." She giggled, and the sound filled me with joy. On the entire ride up to Buttercup Lake, I'd feared how Daisy would take it.

Anger. Confusion… never wanting to see me again.

But as I watched her process the news, her expression only seemed to soften with each passing minute.

She scowled. "So, did Nick think Tate was his?"

I nodded, taking a sip of coffee. "It sounds like he did at first but then started to hesitate as Tate got older. Brielle had mentioned he saw an old photo of me on her phone and had a heart-to-heart talk with her about things, especially the timing of things.

Daisy grimaced. "Yikes."

I nodded. "Yeah, it could have gone south really quickly. But Nick understood and felt like they hadn't been serious enough to warrant getting after her, but he did ask for a paternity test, and he knew Tate wasn't his."

"This is all just mind-blowing." She shook her head. "Like, I can't even believe that you have a son."

I continued, "I'm sorry I didn't tell you sooner. I needed time to process it myself. I just never expected to hear I had a son. I'm still trying to wrap my head around being a dad and what that will mean."

She nodded, studying me. But she didn't say anything.

"I didn't feel like it was something to just text you or tell you over the phone, either."

Daisy smiled, her eyes staying locked on mine. "I appreciate that, and I'll confess that having some schnapps in my morning mocha has probably taken the edge off."

I laughed, glancing at Abby. "Maybe I ought to try a little of that too. These last couple of days have been some of the best of my life, but I can't stop worrying about losing you. This is a lot to ask of you."

She reached across the table, her hand gently covering mine.

"I plan to be a very involved parent, and we're just

starting our relationship. I won't blame you if—"

"We both said we saw a future with lots of kids." She drew a deep breath. "We're just starting early. You know, before we even say the L word."

"No, Daisy. I love you. I'm saying it right now." I laughed, shaking my head. "In between taking in Tate's little arms and legs and his coos… all I wanted to do was share it with you. I missed having you there so badly, it hurt."

"Really?"

I nodded. "The only thing that would have made finding out I was a dad better was finding it out with you."

Relief washed over her, and she nodded. "I held onto the hope that what we'd shared was magical that night, and I just knew in my heart that this was my Christmas of Love. I could see it in your eyes, and to know that now I have even more of you to love…" She smiled. "Just melts my heart, and I love you, Hunter Knox, and Tate too."

"I was so afraid I'd lose you," I confessed.

A smile tipped her lips. "You won't ever lose me. I'm impossible to shake."

The door opened widely as the sound of jingles exploded into the coffee shop. I spotted an overly enthusiastic elf wandering in, setting his sights on our table and ringing his bells with gusto.

"Be careful. The elf is a little tipsy. He already tripped over a table earlier."

I snickered as the elf's gaze found mine and he scowled.

The elf made his way over. "You'd better be good to our Daisy, Hunter."

I frowned, trying to see through the makeup. "Nate? Is that you?"

I could smell the peppermint Schnapps rolling off his breath and smiled.

"Yeah. It's me, but don't let this costume fool ya. I'll make your holidays a living hell if you break her heart."

Daisy chuckled. "It pays to have friends in high places."

"That's right, Daisy. Never fear, the elf is here." Nate winked at her, and I couldn't help but like the guy.

Maybe my brothers were right about him. He wasn't so bad if he wanted to protect Daisy's heart, but that was my job now.

And then a thought occurred to me.

Amy.

Chapter Twenty-Three

Daisy

The door to my cozy home creaked open. The frosty night air spilled into the warm living room filled with the glow of Christmas lights. Hunter came in right behind me, holding the cat carrier with angry meows emanating from inside.

"Welcome to the North Pole," I joked, gesturing at my overly festive decorations. In my frantic attempt at ignoring the Brielle rumors, I'd pulled out every single piece of Christmas décor I'd ever purchased and created my own winter wonderland.

Hunter chuckled, setting down the carrier. "Looks like you've been busy since I was last here."

"It's called pretending everything is just fine while you're secretly worried your world is crashing down." She flashed a wry grin. "But don't worry. I'm totally fine."

Hunter smiled, shaking his head. "I wish I had just answered Brielle while you were there, and then you could have been there with me when I found out about Tate."

His words stirred warmth through me, but I shook my head. "It all happened the way it was supposed to. I promise."

The cat emerged with aristocratic grace from her carrier. Purrlock's gaze swept the room, landing on the fireplace with a flicker of feline interest.

I headed to the kitchen, my voice trailing behind. "How about some hot cocoa?"

"Make it extra chocolatey," he called after me, his voice rich and warm. It was as if the hecticness from the last few days all vanished the moment he was here.

"Sounds good. Will you turn on some Christmas tunes?"

He nodded, turning on the fireplace and reaching for the remote as Purrlock Holmes investigated her new surroundings.

In the kitchen, the waltz of hot cocoa making began. I reached for a pan, grabbed some milk and cocoa, and looked over at Hunter, who'd already settled in on my couch. Having him here made things feel like home. Or maybe it was just Hunter who felt like home, my home.

I pondered that last thought as a symphony of spoons clinking against mugs and milk whirring in the pot took my focus. I didn't want to burn anything tonight. I looked up and noticed Hunter leaning against the wall, watching me with a sweet smile that was part amusement… and maybe something deeper.

"Careful," I teased, catching his glance. "You might start believing I'm a cocoa aficionado."

"I wouldn't dare doubt it," he replied, the corners of his eyes crinkling.

"Imagine little Tate here when he's older, drinking some cocoa out of a sippy cup."

Hunter grinned, his gaze staying focused on mine. "I'd like to believe that by then, we were cohabiting in the same place."

I chuckled and pointed the spoon at him. "Ah, good call."

With two steaming mugs in hand, we settled into the living room. Purrlock perilously perched herself on the mantel, eyeing the stockings with a predator's focus.

It had me concerned, but I wasn't about to ruin this moment with Hunter. Not after the last few days of emotional upheaval.

Hunter chuckled. "Looks like someone's making a bid for Santa's naughty list."

I laughed. "Or trying to assert dominance."

"I wouldn't want to see that fight." He grinned as I rolled my eyes.

We sipped our cocoa as Christmas carols echoed softly through the house. The rich chocolate was a perfect antidote to the winter chill, not to mention the days spent worrying about things I didn't even want to believe. The roiling fire and the twinkling Christmas lights cast a warm, intimate glow around us.

I turned to look at Hunter and smiled. "At least you've had practice with Purrlock."

He shrugged, a grin tugging at his lips. "And it's been a mostly paws-itive experience."

"Seriously?" I smirked.

"Would you expect anything less from a guy who names his cat Purrlock?"

"Good point."

"It's all part of my charm," he said, his eyes sparkling with mischief.

"Unfortunately, you're right." I bopped his nose as Purrlock licked her paws four feet up from the ground.

I pulled a festive blanket covered in gingerbread houses onto our laps.

"And think, this time last week, I thought it was just you, me, and a furball," he mused, his tone a mix of humor and earnestness.

"Life is full of adventure." I nodded. "What's that thing people say? You plan, and God laughs?"

"Truer words." He nodded, pulling my hand into his as Purrlock kept tabs on us.

"I like what I see for our future," Hunter said as my heart skipped a beat.

"Me too," I confessed.

Suddenly, a clatter from the fireplace drew our attention. The cat, in a display of feline acrobatics, had leaped from the mantel, but her tail got stuck, and she wound up hanging upside down in front of the fire, yowling as if the world had set her up for this.

A stocking fell, catching on her claw as Hunter shot up from the couch.

"I'm sorry. Can you just?" I shouted between laughter, grabbing my phone.

Hunter laughed as I took a couple of photos of Purrlock.

"Get in there."

Hunter knelt next to his cat and turned around with a grimace just as I took the perfect holiday shot.

"Operation Santa Paws is a go." He laughed, shaking his head as he lifted poor Purrlock back onto the mantel before untangling her tail from the fireplace vent.

I watched the way Hunter interacted with the cat. Gentle and patient. It was in these small moments that I saw our potential, not just as a couple but as something more—a family in the making.

And I knew he was going to make a dynamite dad to Tate.

Hunter returned, his eyes meeting mine. "Where were we?" he asked, a playful note in his voice. "Wasn't I about to kiss you?"

The familiar pull of electricity shot through me.

"I think so," I said more breathlessly than I thought as he closed the gap between us. Our lips met in a gentle kiss, but it was charged with all the unspoken words and shared laughter of the evening. And I knew Hunter really was my home.

In my cozy living room, the glow of the Christmas tree lights cast a soft, warm hue over us.

Hunter's lips slowly broke away, and he smiled with a heated look in his gaze. "I forgot how incredible those lips of yours are."

I grinned, touching them. "I try to keep them moisturized with candy-cane lip balm," I joked.

"Don't stop."

"Want more cocoa?"

He nodded, and I took his mug, filling it to the top.

We nestled back on the sofa, the shared gingerbread blanket draped over our laps. The air was scented with the essence of pine trees and the subtle hint of the cinnamon potpourri on the coffee table.

He held his hot cocoa as the lazy swirls of steam rose from the mug. I watched, amused, as he blew gently on it, his eyes flicking up to meet mine with a playful challenge.

"I do not know why that is turning me on, but it is." I laughed, shaking my head. "I'm doomed. I'm a hot mess around you."

"I'm flattered." He puffed another poof of air onto the steam and smiled.

His shoulders touched mine as he sipped his drink, and I couldn't deny that the attraction was as strong as ever. I couldn't wait to enlighten the Sunshine Breakfast Club.

"So," I began a bit more seriously. "What do you think your first Christmas season with your son will be like?"

He pondered my question, a small smile playing on his lips. "I imagine a lot of early mornings and late nights. I can just picture his big eyes staring at a pile of Christmas presents he doesn't have a clue what to do with." There was a hopeful glint in his eyes, one that made my heart flutter. "But above all, I just can't wait to hold him. To sit on the couch next to you while Purrlock glares—I mean, stares—at us."

"That sounds amazing, Hunter."

He turned to look at me and nodded. "I just hope I haven't scared you off."

"It takes more than a crazy cat and a cute baby boy to do that."

We fell into a comfortable silence, our eyes often meeting and holding. It was crazy how our gaze spoke volumes without the need for words. It was like that with my mom and my brother. We just knew.

Without warning, a loud beeping sound from outside blared into our perfect little abode. "Ugh. Not again," I groaned, glancing at Hunter.

"What's that?" He shook his head, unsure of what I was talking about.

"For the last few days, there's been nothing but loud trucks beeping back and forth and movers bringing all kinds of things to the house across the street. I guess it's safe to say someone is moving in."

I hopped off the couch and went into my kitchen to get a better view. Sure enough, a white moving van from some furniture store was pulling in backward.

"Whoever it is, they're only filling up their house with new furniture. Extra fancy." I grinned at Hunter. "Maybe you could sell your SUV to them. I bet they'd like the heated seats."

Hunter grinned, and the way his eyes crinkled at the corners made my heart skip a beat. He scratched his head and laughed nervously.

"What?" My hand flew to my hip.

He set his mug on the coffee table, turning to face me fully. His gaze was intense, filled with uncertainty.

"There's one more thing." His lip twisted into a sexy pout, but when I met his gaze, the weight of his words dug into me.

"What?" My brows knitted together.

Hunter made his way over to me in the kitchen. He reached out, tucking a stray lock of hair behind my ear. His touch lingered, sending tingles through me.

Maybe whatever it was, it wasn't so bad after all.

I felt my cheeks warm, a delightful mix of shyness and excitement churning through me. "Spit it out."

He let out a deep breath and moved his hands to my shoulders as if to anchor me in place. "Nick and Brielle bought that house to be closer to me."

I opened my mouth to say something funny, witty, or... Well, nothing came except the realization that my world just got a lot bigger. I closed my mouth and let out a long sigh as I realized what this meant.

Our eyes locked, and in that moment, everything else faded away. It was just us wrapped in the warmth of my home, the Christmas lights, and the possibilities of our shared future that kept growing by the minute. The seriousness of our conversation was balanced by the playful spark between us. It created the perfect blend of complexity and lightness, but one thing I was certain of was that this had become the Christmas of Love.

And there wasn't much more to say.

Chapter Twenty-Four

Hunter

In the heart of a snowy afternoon, I dusted my gloves off, surrounded by Christmas decorations that sparkled like jewels against the white blanket of snow. I'd just put up a display in front of Daisy's house as a large moving truck backed into the drive across the street.

I glanced at Daisy peering outside, giving me a thumbs-up sign before waggling her brows. I made my way back inside, and she wrapped her arms around me like she hadn't seen me for weeks, and I loved every second of it.

My son was coming in tonight with Nick and Brielle,

271

and I couldn't wait to introduce Daisy to him. A honk blared outside as a curious spectacle unfolded. I let Daisy go, and we turned to look out the kitchen window. Daisy handed me a cup of coffee as the passenger side door of the truck swung open, and out stepped my ex-girlfriend, complete with oversized sunglasses and a fur coat that screamed Beverly Hills more than Wisconsin.

"Guess who's here?" Daisy joked, her tone laced with a mix of amusement and incredulity. Her eyebrows shot up as she recognized her. "She knows how to make a statement, but where's Tate?"

I shook my head, wondering the same thing. I didn't spot Nick, but I knew they were flying in together on his jet.

"Well, that's definitely Brielle in all her glory," I confirmed, watching as she directed the movers with the flair of a Broadway director.

"Should we go say hi?" Daisy joked, a playful glint in her eyes.

I snorted. "Sure, right after I learn to fly. When Brielle's in a mood like that, I know to stay away."

Daisy took a sip of wine and grinned as we watched Brielle battling a gust of icy wind. "She knows how that's going to end, right?"

I shook my head, staring. "I don't think so."

272

Brielle attempted to secure her hat while simultaneously navigating a path through the snow in heels that were definitely not snow-friendly.

"Her shoes are going to be the death of her," Daisy mused. "You might get full custody after all."

I couldn't help but laugh, shaking my head in dismay. "I remember her having a thing for impractical footwear."

The scene was like a sitcom, complete with us being the nosy neighbors peeking through our window, but I couldn't help myself.

"What if this is her secret plan?" Daisy asked, half-joking, half-serious. "Move up to northern Wisconsin and have her way with you."

I took her hand, squeezing it gently. "Even if it was, it wouldn't change a thing. You're the one I want. Besides, she absolutely hates it here. From what I could tell, this was Nick's idea. I'd be surprised if she shows up less and less when I have Tate."

She smiled, reassured by my words. "Good answer. You just earned yourself some of my famous Christmas cookies."

I looked out the window to see Brielle struggling with a large box, and then the bottom gave way, sending a cascade of high heels onto the snowy driveway.

We couldn't help but laugh.

"I feel so guilty," Daisy said, shaking her head. "I mean, she always looked at me like a bug she wanted to squash with one of those shoes, but this is next-level."

"Should we help her?" I asked, still chuckling.

"Let's do it," Daisy said empathically. "But first, let me grab some boots for her. I think Brielle could use a pair."

She found a pair of sturdy boots with fur poking out the top and grinned at me. "They'll match her coat."

Arm in arm, we braved the cold, crossing the street to help Brielle. Surprise filled her gaze when she spotted us for the first time... ever. She seemed grateful for the assistance.

"Wisconsin winters, huh?" Daisy said, picking up a rogue stiletto. "They're a bit unpredictable."

Brielle laughed, a sound that was genuine and warm. "You're telling me! I think I'll need to invest in some boots."

Daisy handed her a pair. "I'm size eight. I hope these will work for you."

Brielle's brows rose in surprise. "Wow. Thanks. I really appreciate it."

I smiled at Daisy, impressed with the woman I fell in love with and grateful for the growth that Brielle somehow experienced from some sort of Christmas miracle. There were no sketchy snarls or stinky stares at Daisy, unlike last year, and I felt like I could let out a sigh of relief.

Maybe.

Or was Brielle up to something?

As we helped her, the tension dissolved into laughter, and we shared stories about winter mishaps from Daisy's point of view.

Standing there, in the midst of a snowy Wisconsin street, surrounded by Christmas decorations and a sense of a Christmas miracle, it was hard to hold onto any animosity.

The holiday spirit seemed determined to bring us together.

One of the movers came over to talk to Brielle, so we waved goodbye and headed back to Daisy's warm home.

As we started back across the street, Brielle called out, "Wait up! Can I invite myself over for coffee? I could use some local wisdom about surviving a Wisconsin winter."

Daisy and I exchanged a worried look, but we made a silent agreement between us.

"Sure, Brielle. Come on over," Daisy said with a grin.

Inside Daisy's cozy living room, with the fireplace crackling and the scent of freshly baked cookies in the air, the atmosphere thawed further. Brielle perched herself on the sofa. It was hard to miss her blaring glamor stark against Daisy's eclectic Christmas décor. The crazy contrast somehow added to the charm of the moment.

"So, you're the bartender who was hot after my boyfriend," Brielle began, her tone friendly while dripping with sarcasm.

That was the Brielle I knew.

"Actually, we had broken up, Brielle."

Daisy shook her head. "Actually, I couldn't stand him last year."

The revelation took the wind right out of Brielle's sails. "Really?"

Daisy pretended to shiver. "Oh, yeah. He was so cocky and ignored me just to get his point across."

"Then how'd you two…?"

Daisy smiled. "The Sunshine Breakfast Club, I think. And a restaurant fire. And Foxy."

Brielle finally shoved her sunglasses on top of her head. "Foxy?"

I laughed, pouring a cup of coffee.

"My Subaru out front. You might have seen her."

Brielle sipped her coffee, her eyes scanning the room. "You know, I never pictured him settling down in a place like this. It's… cozy."

"It grows on you, kind of like me," Daisy replied, handing Brielle a plate of cookies. "I promise I won't bite, and

I'll support your and Hunter's wishes when it comes to Tate. I'm not a bad person, Brielle."

Brielle's demeanor shifted slightly. "I have to admit, I was a bit nervous moving here, especially right down the street from you," she confessed to me. "I was worried it might be... awkward." Brielle shook her head. "And now that I know your girlfriend lives across the street..."

"Serendipity?" Daisy laughed.

Brielle groaned. "Yeah. Let's call it that."

"It's a small world," Daisy said, "But hey, it's always good to have a friend in the neighborhood."

Brielle's eyes softened. "Friend, huh? I'd like that."

I glanced at my phone and brought my gaze to Brielle's. "So, where are Tate and Nick?"

"Well, our designer screwed up, and I had to go hunt down Tate's crib in Portage at some distribution center so that when they got here tonight, he'd have a place to sleep."

"Ah, I got it." I chuckled. Imagine if poor Tate had to sleep on a normal crib like at my house. "Well, at least you found it."

Daisy's doorbell rang, and she hopped up to answer it.

Immediately, Millie's voice rang through the air.

"Dagnabbit. I didn't want to believe it, but the

horrendous rumors must be true." Millie shook her head, pointing over her shoulder. "There's even a moving truck."

Daisy was shaking her head and waving her hands, trying to warn Millie, but she was on a roll. "You hold your man tight because it sounds like Miss Hollywood is back in town. And she's moving across from you, no doubt. What are the odds?"

Daisy turned around to beg me for help. Her cheeks flushed a lovely shade of peach.

"Umm, now's not a good time, Millie," she tried again.

"Oh, hogwash. Hey, Hunter." Millie's eyes bounced from Hunter to Brielle, and she flinched from the recognition.

Brielle smiled and nodded. "At least it's out in the open."

Millie eyed Brielle before bringing her gaze back to Daisy.

"You know what they say," she whispered, elbowing me. "Keep your friends close and your enemies closer. Good play, Daisy. Good play."

"It isn't quite like that, Millie." Daisy looked mortified, but the truth hurt. If Brielle had been kinder to the people of Buttercup Lake, Millie wouldn't have been so protective of Daisy.

But Brielle picked on every single thing that most of us adored about our small town.

Daisy cleared her throat. "Would you like to come in for some cookies?"

"No, I've made enough of a mess of things, dear. You have fun tonight, and just remember, snakes slither until they attack."

"Okay there, Millie. You're just a fountain full of great advice." Daisy gave Millie a hug before she trundled out of the house.

Brielle laughed nervously, shaking her head. "I have a lot of making up to do, it seems."

Daisy shrugged. "I think if you let yourself enjoy the little things, you'll really fall in love with this place, and it will show. Just be kind, really."

"I tend to enjoy sarcasm and cynicism, but I'll try my best." She laughed, looking around Daisy's home.

Brielle's phone buzzed, and she glanced down. "Movers have placed the furniture. I should go over and make sure they didn't screw it up."

Daisy traded a glance with me, and I hid a smile as Brielle made her way to the door. "I'll call you tonight as soon as Nick gets in."

I nodded as Brielle left Daisy's home and shut the

door behind her.

Daisy let out a grunt and leaned back against the door. "That could have gone so poorly. Other than Millie, things went great."

I chuckled. "Can't really blame her, though."

Daisy pushed herself from the door and groaned. "I honestly can't believe that Brielle is moving in across the street."

"Surprise," I teased.

She chuckled. "Life has been nothing but surprises lately."

I nodded, pulling her into my arms. "These surprises almost make me not want to go outside any longer."

"Is that what we should call them?"

I laughed, watching Brielle make her way to the other side of the street, and breathed a sigh of relief.

Daisy wrapped her arms around me, too, and nestled in. "One thing's for sure. I wouldn't want to navigate them with anyone but you."

Chapter Twenty-Five

Daisy

I'd finished the book for the Sunshine Breakfast Club, and tonight was the last official meeting before Christmas. Tonight was also the night I'd get to meet Tate. I walked into the lobby of the community center filled with the familiar Christmas decorations and laughter from down the hall. I shuddered as I walked by the room with the Santa debacle and stayed course for the Sunshine Breakfast Club.

The room hummed with holiday cheer. Twinkling lights festooned every pole, window, and archway, and tables of food were spread as far as the eye could see. I'd brought more of my famous fudge to add to the pile. Ornaments twirled merrily from the ceiling, basking in the cozy glow of Christmas lights, and I didn't think the place could get any cuter.

A majestic Christmas tree stood in the corner, its branches laden with handmade decorations and silver tinsel. Everything was perfect, and for once, I didn't want to run in the other direction from the festivities.

The aromas of spiced cider and freshly baked treats circulated through the air, and it felt so good to be on this side of the Sunshine Breakfast Club's plans. Hunter and I had made it over the hurdle, even if no one else knew it.

Although, I suppose if things went horribly tonight, Hunter could think twice about things.

But I loved kids. I wanted a gaggle of kids. Might as well start now.

I glanced at the dessert table, which was adorned with an array of festive delights, and my stomach growled. A glorious Yule log, dusted with powdered sugar and inlaid with vibrant red berries and holly leaves, added a pop of color to the center of the table.

Next to the holiday cake were tiny pecan and cherry pies with their flaky, buttery crusts. Sprinkle cookies and rugelach lined each side of the table. It became clear that I'd have to be rolled out of here. I spotted a tray of gingerbread cookies, artfully decorated with red icing to resemble tiny Santas, and snagged one.

"So, tell us everything! How's it going with Hunter?" Maya asked, sneaking up behind me.

I nearly dropped my Santa cookie when Millie came up on the other side of me. "And that Brielle? What's going on there?"

I laughed as a blush crept up my cheeks. "Well, it's been wonderful, actually. I knew I was right about him."

Millie's eyes twinkled. "About what?"

"Keeping the faith, having hope."

She smiled and nodded. "You were right, but for the record, I'm rarely wrong."

"You weren't wrong this time, either. Hunter is the one for me."

"But I can't believe the ex moved in across from you. She hates it here. She hates us. Drama… she is full of drama!" chimed in Abby, her tone laced with a playful note as she popped a sprinkle cookie in her mouth.

The truth was that nobody here knew about little Tate, but Hunter told me that tonight, I should tell them. His mom would be here in a little bit and would support me however was needed.

"Yeah, that was quite a surprise," I admitted, recounting the evening when Brielle came over for coffee after her box of Dior slingbacks spilled onto her snowy driveway. "But it turned out to be a sweet visit. I mean, there were a couple of glimpses of the old Brielle, but I think she's been through a lot. She's…" What was the word Hunter used? "Softened. Who knows? Maybe we'll even become friends."

I looked at the ladies in front of me, and I couldn't tell whether they wanted to laugh or cry.

Maya squeezed my hand. "Only you could turn a potentially awkward situation into a budding friendship."

"Not awkward," Millie muttered. "That's more like World War Three in my book."

Hunter's mom walked into the room, and the moment her eyes met mine, it felt like the weight of the world had lifted.

I respected her now more than ever. Once Hunter told me his mom was the only person who knew, and she refused to tell a soul, I knew we'd be close.

Amid the laughter and chattering, I beelined over to her.

She gave me a quick hug and shook her head. "I'm dying to meet Tate. What about you?"

I nodded. "Tonight's the night."

"So, what time do we dash out of here?" Her eyes sparkled with the same excitement I felt.

"Hunter said that Brielle and Nick were coming over to his house with Amy and Tate at seven o'clock."

She squeezed my arms and smiled. "Perfect. That gives me time to go home and freshen up. I've spent all day shopping for my grandson."

I smiled, nodding. "You sound like Hunter."

Being surrounded by friends, good food, and the magic of the holiday season made me realize that Hunter was right. In order to embrace the new memories and good times, I had to make peace with the old ones. It was a process, but with every step forward, I felt lighter and brighter.

And I felt hope.

I looked around the cozy winter wonderland as ladies bonded by friendships, stories, and laughter made the world a better place. And maybe, one day, I could even trick Brielle into getting into the fold.

Until then, I knew what my new plan was going to be. I just had to wait until the right time to bring it up.

I followed Maya, Nina, and Millie to the food line, picking up a plate and piling it high with salads, wings, quiche, and more before sitting on a chair next to the tree. Hunter's mom sat next to me with a mischievous glint in her eyes.

"I absolutely love surprises." She flashed a wry grin.

"So, Hunter redeemed himself," Millie said, taking a seat next to the table of desserts.

Hunter's mom smiled and shook her head. "He never needed to."

"True story," I said, chuckling. "He's an incredible man."

The book club members hushed as all eyes fell on me. I felt my cheeks warm under their gazes. "It's true, and I always knew it."

"I hate to ask, and since his mom's here, it's not like I'm doing it behind anyone's back, but…" Millie eyed me. "What was he doing at a hotel with Brielle?"

Hunter's mom slid her hand to mine and squeezed it.

I drew a breath and nodded. "Fair question, and I know it comes from a place of caring for me."

Maya nodded and glanced at her grandmother. "Absolutely."

"But you didn't answer my question, dear," Millie said softly, and I realized she cared fiercely for the women she matched.

Hunter's mom nodded.

I drew a breath. "He was meeting his son."

The room quieted as everyone's gazes dropped to their plates of food.

"It's true," Hunter's mom confirmed. "I'm an extremely happy grandmother."

Without missing a beat, Millie sprang from her chair, dumping her plate of food on the floor, and clapped her hands. "Now that makes perfect sense."

"It does?" I cocked my head.

I'd had a lot of reactions, but that wasn't one of them when I found out.

"This is incredible news." Millie lit up the room as she came over, hugged Hunter's mom, and glanced at me. "And you're going to make the best stepmom."

"Whoa, slow down there, Millie." I grinned, taking a bite of the gingerbread Santa but relishing in her compliment because, as of now, I just felt in over my head.

"So that's why Brielle moved to town?" Nina asked.

I nodded. "That's why she came over too. I still didn't expect to invite her in for coffee on day one, but it was a relief."

Nina leaned in, her eyes wide with intrigue. "Come on. Was there a dramatic showdown?"

I smiled, shaking my head. "I swear. I was telling the truth earlier. Actually, we ended up bonding over our shared love for terrible reality TV shows. She's not so bad. And the nanny sounds amazing."

"Nanny?" Millie asked.

"Yup. She has more than one, but Amy is who will be here in Buttercup Lake the most, helping with Tate." I looked around at the ladies and drew a deep breath. There was something addicting about this little club of ours. "I think I found our next match."

Millie gasped and looked at all the members. "Who?"

"Amy." I cleared my throat. "Amy and Nate."

"The elf?" Abby grinned, and I chuckled.

"I think we should introduce him as the sheriff first."

She winked at me. "Good call."

"So, you're serious?" Millie asked, intrigued.

I nodded. "It was actually Hunter's idea."

"Wow. I was worried I was running out of people." Millie looked surprised.

Abby and Maya had already cleaned up the mess on the floor and handed Millie a second plate as she took a seat. "Then we have a lot of work to do. We'd better get on it."

As I sat surrounded by the magic of the Christmas season and our quaint little book club, I realized how much my life had changed for the better since letting myself believe in the idea of love. And thanks to Hunter, I didn't have to let loss define me any longer. I smiled, grateful for the love, friendship, and unexpected surprises that had come my way because of these women and the Sunshine Breakfast Club.

The planning session ended right on time, and I made my way home and parked Foxy in the drive. There was something different about the way she drove lately, and I hoped she'd make it through another winter.

I trudged through the freshly fallen snow to my front door, which Hunter quickly opened. The crisp winter air nipped at my cheeks, and I couldn't help but replay the evening in my mind. The Sunshine Breakfast Club's party had been a delightful blur of delicious treats, laughter, and stories filled with hope that warmed you from the inside out. Yet, amid the festive cheer, my thoughts kept drifting back to us— to Hunter and me.

When Hunter opened his arms wide, a flutter of excitement stirred in my belly. Purrlock wrapped her tail around his ankle as she purred.

"Bringing a date, I see," I teased, my heart dancing merely from seeing Hunter.

"She insisted," he replied with his lopsided grin that never failed to quicken my pulse. "And you know I can never win with her."

"Seems to be a theme with the females in your life.

It's good that you have a son."

Hunter kissed me on my cheek. "I love you so much."

"I love you too."

Purrlock walked back inside and settled on the rug. A mischievous spark ignited in her eyes. Before we could react, she leaped toward the mantel again… this time, knocking over a Santa figurine. Hunter dove like a quarterback and caught it in his hands.

"She is quite a handful," he muttered.

"Purrlock gets it from her owner," I joked as he stood back up and set the figurine on the mantel.

Hunter closed the gap between us. His blue eyes held mine with an intensity that made my heart race.

The air between us crackled with unspoken hopes and dreams, the kind of thoughts that linger on the tip of your tongue, but they never quite find their way into the world. There was something about sharing the unspoken with Hunter that made me feel like we could conquer anything in the world.

Surrounded by the cozy trimmings of my living room, everything felt intensified. Between the soft glow of the Christmas lights, the flickering of the fireplace, and the way his gaze saw right to my soul, I never wanted this Christmas season to end.

This was the first Christmas since my brother and mom passed away where I felt like I could breathe again, that there was hope.

And that hope lived in love.

His fingers softly brushed away some curls from my shoulder. "I want you to know that I'm truly, deeply in love with you, Daisy. I know you're about to meet my son, but I want you to know that our family can just keep growing."

My mind raced as I nodded. With each new day, it felt like his family was growing, and the thought that he wanted me to be a part of it warmed me to my soul.

When Brielle arrived, a hurricane of insecurities flooded through me, and most of them I didn't even realize had existed, but Hunter supported me, and I saw the sincerity in his eyes. We would make this work, no matter what the future held for us all.

"It's always been you, Daisy. The moment I saw you when I came to Buttercup Lake last fall... I could barely think straight. And then when I hired you at the bar..." He shook his head. "I just knew you were the one."

"All I wanted was a kiss," I teased. "And now..."

"You've got a lot more than you bargained for." We stood quietly, basking in the warmth of the fireplace, holding on to distant hopes and dreams.

"Are you ready to meet my son?"

"More than ready."

We stood there, basking in the warmth of shared excitement and unspoken promises. The enchantment of Christmas wove around us, binding us together in a tapestry of hope and new beginnings.

Chapter Twenty-Six

Hunter

I let out a deep breath as Daisy glanced in my direction. We'd arrived at my house just in time. The caterers were working away in the kitchen. I looked over at Daisy as a cocktail of emotions swept through me. It was hard to fathom that today, my girlfriend, my parents, and my ex and her fiancé would be under the same roof, my roof, united by my son, the scrumptious, cooing bundle of joy I still couldn't believe was mine.

The doorbell rang, and Daisy stepped closer as I opened it to see Nick, Brielle, and Amy holding Tate. The nanny's eyes connected with mine, and I immediately held my son close.

A small gasp only I could hear escaped Daisy's lips as her gaze locked onto Tate's. Daisy's expression lit up in a mixture of tenderness and admiration, and my heart actually swelled.

"It's so good to see you again, Daisy." Brielle gave her a quick air kiss on each side as Nick stepped forward to shake her hand.

"Thanks for lending my fiancée some boots. She's already placed an order from Neiman Marcus." He grinned as Daisy laughed.

"I'm just glad she didn't go down along with the rest of her belongings."

"Indeed."

"Come on in," Daisy said, taking over as I stared at my son.

I couldn't wait for my parents to meet him. He definitely had more Knox in him than anything.

I followed behind my guests as Daisy poured them drinks and welcomed them to sit in the living room. Amy stayed behind, but Daisy insisted that she join the rest of us. That was what I loved about Daisy.

Quietly holding Tate, I watched Daisy come toward me, tentatively approaching us. But her gaze never left Tate's as he cooed, staring at the ceiling and completely unaware of the pivotal moment unfolding.

"He's gorgeous," Daisy whispered. I could detect the overwhelming amount of emotion laced in her words. "Just like his father."

I chuckled. "He's got your charm already. I can tell he's gleaming on every word you say."

She grinned and rested her hand on my shoulder. "He's gotta learn from the best."

The doorbell rang, but my mom didn't wait for anyone to answer it as she swept into my home, leaving my dad in the dust, standing on the stoop.

The moment my mom spotted me sitting on the couch, holding Tate, with Daisy behind me, tears brimmed her eyes. Maternal pride oozed from my mom as she walked toward us. My dad came behind her and shook his head slowly in awe.

"You know, he's going to break hearts one day, just like his dad." She winked at me, and Daisy chuckled.

Daisy grinned. "Tell me about it."

I glanced at Brielle and Nick and could tell they had their own rhythm. His hand rested on hers as they watched the scene unfold between our ever-growing family.

"You two did good," my mom said softly, glancing at

Brielle.

There was no denying that the air hung with unspoken words about past hurts from my ex, but Brielle stood and closed the gap between us. "He's got the best of both of us." She pressed her lips into a smile as my parents nodded in agreement.

The frailty of the moment was a delicate balance that laced together old wounds and new beginnings, but at the root of it all was Tate. He bridged the gaps and erased the hurt.

"Would you like to hold Tate?" I asked my mom.

Her eyes lit up as I handed her our little bundle. His red Santa pajamas were enough to do anyone in. My dad chortled as he watched his wife hold their grandson.

I wrapped my arms around Daisy as the aroma of roasted turkey filled the air and the caterers worked away in the kitchen.

Daisy leaned her head against my chest. "This is what life is about, isn't it?"

Her gaze locked on mine as she tipped her chin to see me. "You were right. Hope, new beginnings, love…"

I kissed the top of her head and felt the outpouring of tenderness my girlfriend had for this moment.

My dad was now holding Tate, but his eyes connected with Daisy's. "I think it's your turn."

Daisy's eyes brightened, and I swore I heard a little squeal as my Dad brought him over.

Tate nestled himself in Daisy's arms, and she looked like a natural. She took a seat next to Brielle and rocked him gently. When she looked up at me, her eyes laced with affection, she shook her head and smiled. "He's the most incredible little boy I've ever met."

Brielle smiled with pride and let out a deep breath, patting Daisy's arm. "You're doing so well."

Tightness clamped down on my chest in a whirlwind of emotions. Brielle's words were so simple yet so profound at this moment. She brought her gaze to mine, and it affirmed my decision to bring these crazy worlds together.

As the night wore on, the house echoed with the sounds of shared stories and easy laughter. Tate, continually passed from arm to arm, had more love than I knew possible. Little Tate enjoyed being the star of the show, flirting, hiccupping, and gurgling in wide-eyed wonderment, eliciting adoration from everyone.

And then it happened. He got that dopey smile right when his grandpa held him tight.

I chuckled, shaking my head as Daisy grinned, knowing exactly what that meant.

"Why are you all backing away?" my dad asked.

My mom chuckled as Amy came over with a diaper and wipes. "It's diaper time."

I expected my Dad to hand over Tate immediately, but he grabbed the diaper right out of Amy's hands and chuckled. "It's as easy as riding a bike."

He set Tate on the couch and within an instant had him changed, clothed, and ready to be passed around again.

Brielle stood by the window overlooking the lake where a few Christmas parade boats chugged along the water. The big light parade on the lake wasn't until tomorrow, but there were always a few boats lit up and cruising. I caught her gaze, and she raised her glass in a silent toast. There was no white flag of surrender or a whisper of an apology, but we now shared an appreciation for peace. Daisy walked over to me, and I returned the gesture to Brielle. I knew we might have been lousy partners, but we could navigate this new territory with respect.

"Your parents are in heaven," she whispered, her warm breath skating along my ear.

I wrapped an arm around Daisy, pulling her close to me and depositing another kiss on her head. "A little bit of holiday magic never hurts."

"And the Sunshine Breakfast Club." I eyed Amy. "When should we invite Amy to our Christmas Eve party?"

"I already spoke to Brielle, and she thought it was a great idea."

"Awesome. We'll just do it before they leave tonight."

"I can't believe I'm a willing participant in these shenanigans."

Daisy snorted. "Willing participant? Try ringleader. This was your idea, if I remember correctly."

I flashed a wicked grin. "Look how great it's turned out for us."

My mom walked over to Daisy and handed over Tate. "Do you think this boy will ever feel a crib or stroller again?"

Daisy chuckled and shook her head. "Highly doubtful."

Amy sat on the couch and smiled at us. "It certainly makes my job easy."

I watched my mom motion for Brielle to follow her to the couch near the fireplace. Brielle glanced at me as Nick chatted with the caterers in the kitchen. In the softly lit corner of the living room, away from the holiday cheer, clinking of glasses, and clanging silverware, Brielle and my mom found a quiet space. The Christmas tree with red and green twinkle lights shed a soft light over them.

"What do you think that's about?" Daisy whispered.

"Everything okay?"

I shrugged and took a deep breath. "I hope so."

My mom took Brielle's hand in hers and smiled. "Thank you for allowing us to be a part of Tate's life." My mom's voice was tender but filled with the wisdom and compassion of her years. "Brielle, you've given us a precious gift." Her eyes flicked to Tate, who was now asleep in my girlfriend's arms.

Brielle nodded, her eyes glistening. "I never expected to have a son, not Hunter's son. Not children at all. But I'm so grateful to Nick. He's really shown me how to be kind," she whispered, a mix of pride and vulnerability in her voice. "And Tate is my everything, even if I don't know what to do sometimes or need a million nannies. I love him. I really do."

"You're not alone in this. Tate is a part of this family now. He's a part of us, and by extension, so are you."

Brielle took a deep breath, her shoulders relaxing slightly. "I've been so anxious about everything. How Nick and I will manage, how he'll fit into our lives and your lives."

My mother smiled warmly, dabbing tears away. "Tate is already a part of us, dear. Just like you are. Families come in all sizes and shapes. Ours merely got a little bigger, spicier, and a little more special."

Tears welled in Brielle's eyes as she turned to look at

Tate. "I want what's best for him. I want him to grow up surrounded by love and knowing his family, all of his family, is there for him."

"And that will happen. We will figure things out as they come, together, as a family. It's a blessing."

The genuineness of my mom's words touched Brielle, and I was so grateful that they put everything aside for the sake of Tate.

As I watched from across the room, my heart grew with love and gratitude.

Nick made his way into the living room and announced that dinner was served. We all moved toward the dining table, laden with a scrumptious holiday feast, but none of us wanted to put Tate down. Daisy sat next to me, still holding him in her arms as I put turkey, stuffing, and cranberry sauce on her plate.

"This looks delicious," she muttered, stabbing a piece of stuffing with her fork in her right hand while Tate lay asleep nestled in her left arm.

"She's a natural," Brielle said, laughing. "I still don't think I could do that."

"This is probably my only natural talent," Daisy assured her.

"So, Hunter told me you two are getting married after

Christmas and headed to Bora Bora for the honeymoon?"

Brielle looked suddenly sheepish, but she nodded. "Yeah. It's not the first time I've had to leave Tate, but I know he's in good hands."

My mom smiled, nodding. "Well, it's your honeymoon, dear."

Nick nodded.

As everyone began talking about Bora Bora, I leaned into Daisy, my voice low. "I always thought mistletoe was overrated when I wanted to impress the ladies. So I thought, why not shake things up and go bigger and better with you? You know, impress you by bringing in a baby and an ex for the holidays?"

Daisy snickered and shook her head. "Well, you really outdid yourself."

My dad cleared his throat and grinned at me with a mischievous glint. "Hunter, I must say that this beats watching reruns of *It's A Wonderful Life*. This real life you've created has spice and plenty of adventure, but I confess I never would have guessed that you'd bring us a grandson for Christmas. Our little Tate is quite a gift, but I think I can only handle one of your surprises per holiday, Hunter."

Everyone laughed, and I shook my head. "Just wait until my brothers meet Tate."

Daisy nodded. "Maya and Nina are going to be worse than we are with hugging him."

Hunter nodded and raised his glass. "To unexpected gifts, new traditions, and a Christmas full of love. May our holidays always be this lively."

"To family," my mom added.

"To family," we all announced.

"Oh, and Amy," Daisy started, turning her attention to the poor, unsuspecting nanny. "We'd love to have you over on Christmas Eve. We're having a little get-together, and since Nick and Brielle will be out of town, we thought it would be perfect."

Amy lit up and nodded. "That sounds amazing. Thank you."

"Absolutely." Daisy grinned. "We look forward to it."

The dining room filled with the low murmur of voices, the sound of glasses clanking, and laughter as we stuffed our bellies and passed Tate around.

Despite the unexpected turns and surprises, this Christmas season felt truly magical.

By the end of the evening, it had been decided that Tate would stay at my house, and I'd call Amy if I needed anything.

As the caterers, my family, and Amy, Brielle, and Nick shuffled into the crisp winter night, the house fell into a peaceful rhythm, which was a complete contrast to the lively commotion earlier.

There we were, just the two of us and Tate. Daisy rested her head on my shoulder as I stared at my son, peacefully asleep in his crib. The baby camera and monitor had been set up to alert me of his every move, but I was still apprehensive to leave.

But I knew he would be fine. I hugged Daisy and brought her closer as I watched my son sleep. I'd been waiting for what felt like forever for this, and I couldn't thank Brielle enough for going on her honeymoon soon.

"Quite a night, huh?" I whispered.

She nodded, giving me a hug as I watched Daisy, who'd joined Tate to become the center of my universe. She linked her hands with mine as we walked down the hall to the living room.

Daisy curled up on the couch, with her fabulous smile glowing at me and her hazel eyes reflecting the flickering lights of the fireplace. I sat down next to her and let out an exhausted sigh.

She let out a soft laugh, turning to face me after my sigh. "Understatement of the year. I never imagined I'd be spending the holidays like this. But, you know, in a strangely beautiful way."

Her hand linked with mine, fingers intertwining naturally. "I can't believe how well you handled everything. The baby, your ex, the family drama… You're amazing, you know that?"

"Having you here makes it all seem manageable. More than that, it feels right." My eyes locked on hers, and I felt that familiar pull to hold Daisy in my arms.

"You always know what to say." Daisy's eyes softened, and she scooted closer. "I've been thinking about our future a lot lately. All the holiday cheer and tonight's chaos made me realize how much I want this."

I nodded, knowing exactly what she meant.

"I want us. I want a life together. It's scary and unpredictable, but when I look at you, I feel like we can handle anything."

"I know it's been a whirlwind, but with you, it feels like I'm exactly where I'm supposed to be." I shook my head. "And Tate feels like the center."

She nodded happily as Purrlock rested in front of the fireplace. She hadn't moved much since Tate showed up, but I think that was her way of adjusting.

"I love you, Hunter Knox," she whispered, crawling

onto my lap.

"I love you too."

I moved my hand to her head and pulled her lips down to mine, kissing her hard.

She let out a little whimper of happiness, and I knew tonight was only the beginning.

Chapter Twenty-Seven

Daisy

On Christmas Eve, Hunter Knox's home buzzed with festive energy. The three Knox brothers, each with their own unique personality, engaged in traditional holiday ribbing, much to the amusement of their dad.

I felt so privileged to be part of such an amazing family, and I was thrilled that Millie, Jackson Jr. and Sr., Carter, Maya, Grace, Izzy, and Nina all showed up.

But the clock was ticking on Nate. He was supposed to be here already.

"Alright, alright," Maya said, watching her husband,

307

Cash, rough-house with Beckett, the oldest Knox brother. Cash's deep, boisterous laugh got the attention of Hunter, who'd been leaning against the fireplace with a mug of hard eggnog in hand.

I walked over to Hunter and waggled my brows. "Hey there, stranger."

He wrapped his arms around my waist and pulled me close. "How are you doing, you sexy little thing?"

I chuckled and shook my head. "I think you've had one too many eggnogs."

He winked at me. "You wish, but in all seriousness, where is Nate?"

"I don't know, but Amy is going to be here any second, and I wanted Nate here first."

As if on cue, the doorbell rang, and Hunter's mom, who was holding Tate, nodded toward the front door for Cash to go open it.

I rushed over to see Amy standing outside, bundled in a silver coat, holding a tray of appetizers.

"Come in," I said, nearly pulling her inside.

I glanced at the tray of tortilla roll-ups and smiled. "You know the way to my heart, Amy."

She grinned as Cash took the tray from her, sliding one of them out to munch on. "And mine, too."

Amy chuckled as I helped her with her coat. "I really can't thank you enough for having me over."

"You are part of the family. Of course."

"How's Tate doing?" she asked, scanning the room and finding him in his grandmother's arms.

"I'd say pretty darn good."

"There's a lot of love in this family," she said softly, and I nodded.

"And the best part is that they don't mind sharing." I winked at her.

Her expression lit up as I closed the door behind her and introduced her to the rest of the family.

Hunter's dad offered her a cranberry fizz, whatever that was, but she happily accepted it as I scanned the time on my phone.

And no message from Nate.

Right when I was about to text him, the door chimed again, and I tried to hide my sloppy grin.

Millie's eyes locked on mine like a wild cat about to feast on its prey, and I chuckled as I walked to the door to see Nate.

"Thank goodness you're not dressed like the elf," I said, teasing.

He took off his cowboy hat and chuckled, still dressed

in his uniform. "I'm sorry for being tardy, but I had to deal with a nuisance call."

My eyes widened. "Give me the deets."

"Two neighbors quarreling down by the hardware store. Apparently, the one neighbor thought it would be funny to hide the other neighbor's life-sized Rudolph in his bed." He shook his head. "While his wife was napping there."

"Boy, you do have your hands full."

"All in a day's work."

I chuckled, shaking my head as Amy turned around to see us.

The moment she saw Nate, I swore I saw lightning flare around her. She dropped her gaze, and I studied Nate to see if I could catch even a glimpse of attraction.

"Okay, everyone. In honor of my new grandson," Hunter's mom proclaimed, "I say we sing *Silent Night*."

"Oh, no," Nate hissed. "I didn't sign up for this."

Amy giggled, and Nate caught her gaze, and I knew the game had begun.

A spark had flickered.

As everyone gathered around the Christmas tree belting out *Silent Night*, Hunter walked over to me and slid his arm around my waist before his mom brought Tate over to us. The song ended, and my heart felt like it was going to burst.

Even in my wildest dreams, I hadn't imagined a Christmas like this again.

Not since I'd lost my brother and mom.

My eyes caught the beginning of the Parade of Boats on the lake, and my heart skipped a beat. It was as if my family were sending me a sign that it was okay to live again.

I drew a deep breath as Hunter led me to the large windows facing the lake as his family gathered behind us. Hunter turned Tate to look at the twinkling Christmas lights parading by us as the most magical feeling sprinkled over me.

I looked up toward the sky and smiled at the brightest star where I was sure my brother and mom were looking down on us, on me.

My expanded family.

As the boat parade ended, I heard Beckett laughing behind us. "Come on, Cash, you've got to admit it, Purrlock here has finally outdone your legendary Christmas tree fiasco of 2007." Beckett laughed, nudging his younger brother.

"What are you talking about?" their mom asked.

Beckett let out a hearty laugh and pointed toward the tree where Purrlock had climbed branch by branch, finally stopping to analyze her mistakes. "That's true. At least when Cash knocked over the tree, he didn't take down half the living room decorations with it."

Hunter cocked his head slightly. "What makes you think that's going to happen?"

"Just a brotherly hunch." He flashed a toothy grin at his brother.

Hunter chuckled, handing me Tate. "Nah, Purrlock knows better."

"I wouldn't do it," Nate said calmly. "Felines have a mind of their own. Let a professional handle it."

Amy nodded in agreement, looking up into Nate's eyes. "Yes, let a professional handle it."

Hunter waved his hand and laughed. "It's okay. I got it."

But he didn't have it.

A loud screech echoed through the air as Purrlock's eyes widened and her mouth opened with a hissing chortle. Without warning, Purrlock used her body like a rocket and leaped toward Hunter, but her reflexes weren't fast enough as he missed her. The cat's body flew like a missile toward the coffee table lined with poinsettias.

"Never a dull moment with you boys." Millie grimaced as Purrlock Holmes's body slid across the table, knocking each plant to the floor before she tumbled right in front of the fireplace.

"Impressive," Cash muttered, shaking his head.

"I think she lost a couple of lives on that one," Millie said, chuckling as Hunter dashed over to check on her.

I quickly followed behind as Purrlock stood slowly and shook off as she stretched her neck toward the ceiling, batting his hand away.

Hunter let out a deep sigh of relief and stood. "The cat is fine. Poinsettias, not so much."

Nate chuckled, shaking his head. "I told you to let a professional handle it."

Hunter grinned and winked at him, patting his shoulder. "Next time, I'll keep that in mind."

Hunter's mom smiled as I held Tate close.

"Welcome to the Knox Christmas Comedy Special, little man," she said, touching her grandson's cheek. "These are your uncles, and for that, I apologize."

Beckett grinned and rolled his eyes. "You know you love us."

She nodded as he hugged her. "And I know Tate is one of you. The apple doesn't fall from the tree in this family."

Cash pretended to be offended, but the twinkle in his blue eyes gave him away. His gaze caught mine, and he motioned for me to come into the hug with Tate, and I found myself swallowed up by the Knox brothers as Hunter came in last.

Tate looked up to see all of his uncles surrounding him, and I knew just how lucky he and I were to join this family.

And then Tate got that dopey smile on his face.

"Ah, how cute," Cash said, touching Tate's chin.

"Look at the little pucker," Beckett said, smiling.

Hunter winked at me, and I picked Beckett. "Here you go, buddy. It's time to hug your little nephew."

Beckett brought him into his arms and hugged him, but a funny look spread across his expression as Nina snickered. "Uh, Nina?"

Her brows rose. "Yeah?"

"I think…" Beckett whistled.

"You think he wasn't as happy to see you as you thought?" Nina chuckled.

Grace brought over a diaper and grinned. "Yeah, that's called gas."

Everyone erupted into laughter, the Christmas cheer running through the room. The Christmas tree still stood tall with only a few ornaments crooked from the fiasco, and I couldn't believe how good it felt to enjoy the holidays again.

The guilt wasn't completely gone, but it didn't burn into me like an ugly reminder like before.

In the midst of the laughter, their mother crossed the room, her eyes gleaming with happiness at the sight of her sons and their loved ones enjoying each other's company. She joined Maya on the sofa, sharing a knowing look that spoke volumes about the pride and love she felt for her family.

As the evening wore on, the teasing subsided, giving way to shared stories of past Christmases, plans for the future, and reflections on the year gone by.

For the first time in years, I felt something growing inside me.

Hope.

I no longer felt the incessant need to make everyone else smile or laugh while I ached inside. I could finally be me.

The room was filled with a sense of togetherness that I belonged to, a testament to the bonds of the Knox family and beyond.

"I never really believed in fate or destiny until I met you. Now, I can't imagine my life without the belief in those things." Hunter's eyes stayed on mine.

"That's the key, Hunter. A belief in something." I rested my head on his shoulder and took in this special scene on Christmas Eve.

We sat there quietly, basking in the warmth from the fireplace. Tate was sleeping soundly in his bedroom while his uncles played Santa Claus.

But I couldn't wait for the real one.

As yawns began circulating from guest to guest, they all left one batch at a time until it was only Hunter and me left, sitting on the couch together, reliving tonight's events.

"Everything has been about me, me, me these last few days, and I want to check in on you," Hunter said, pressing his thumb along my chin while cupping my head softly. "I know the holidays haven't been easy for you since your loss."

I scooted closer and let out a sigh as I snuggled deeper into him. He dropped his arm around me, and I couldn't imagine anywhere else I'd rather be.

"There's something about this year that's been different." I smiled. "A good different. But what I'd give for one more moment with them."

"I'm sorry, baby."

"It's really better this year, though. I just can't put my finger on it."

Hunter smiled, pulling me closer. "I wonder what that could be."

"I have a hunch it's you and the Knox family circus." I sat up, looking into his eyes. "Thank you for reminding me to hope again."

"I did that?" His eyes locked on mine as I nodded.

"You did. I used to think if I enjoyed any part of my life, I was somehow betraying the loss, and eventually, I let grief swallow me up around this time of the year."

"You'll never forget them, but you honor them every day by being you, Daisy. You are an incredible woman."

"You're an incredible man."

He pulled me onto his lap. "I guess we're just two incredible people. Should I go put on my Santa suit?"

I giggled. "Only if I can be your one and only ho-ho-ho."

Hunter laughed, squeezing me tight. "Are you telling me my lines have worn off on you?"

"Did you like it? Was it a good one?" I laughed, resting my head on his chest.

Despite my best efforts, I could feel the sleepiness weigh on me with every passing second.

"You know, I was thinking…"

"Okay, lemme have it."

"I think we need a puppy. I think I'd make a great dog mom. I'll keep her at my house, of course, so we don't irritate Purrlock Holmes."

Hunter's brows quirked. "You want to become a dog mom?"

I nodded. "I think it's a good natural progression."

"You don't think jumping right to Tate already cleared the way for parenthood?"

I chuckled and shrugged. "I don't know. Something just tells me my pup is out there waiting for me."

"Whatever you want, baby." He kissed me softly just as a little bit of fussing came over the monitor.

"Uh-oh." I slid off Hunter's lap as he yawned and stretched while making his way to Tate's room.

I followed quickly behind to see Hunter checking his diaper. As if Hunter had been doing this since his birth, he did a quick swap and walked with Tate in his arms, humming softly as I wandered into Hunter's bedroom.

I climbed into bed, determined to wait up for Hunter.

But then I happily drifted to sleep.

Chapter Twenty-Eight

Hunter

"I can't believe we're doing this." Hunter puffed air in the car and it billowed from his mouth. "Can't we at least turn on some heat while we're doing our stakeout?"

His hand reached for the controls, and I batted it away. "No, we can't give ourselves away. Nate's a police officer, for crying out loud. He knows to look for creepers like us."

I chuckled. "Creepers?"

She shrugged. "I don't know what else to call us."

"How about spies? It sounds more distinguished."

Daisy smiled and let out a happy sigh. "You mean like

007."

"Aren't I the next James Bond?"

She touched my cheek and a thrill ran through me. "Only if I'm your Bond girl."

I blew warm air into my gloved hands and laughed. "Is there any doubt about that? I'm willing to freeze to death in order to help you with your homework assignment."

Daisy rolled her eyes and giggled. "I'm not in school. It's not homework. It's a recon mission. This is what *we* do. And besides, it was your idea to put Amy and Nate together, so you're practically to blame for coming up with this idea."

I smiled as she put the binoculars back up to her eyes. Nate had wandered into the coffee shop, where Abby immediately informed of us his next whereabouts by text. So, here we were, sitting in the parking lot of the Buttercup Lake Recreational Center. We'd been out here for twenty minutes.

In bitter cold temperatures on New Year's Eve.

"A-ha," Daisy squealed. "There he is."

"Yeah?"

"He's got wet hair."

"Okay. That makes sense."

"He must have done some laps, so he likes water. Write that down."

I scowled as she put her binoculars down.

"What am I supposed to write it on?"

"Your phone." She put the binoculars back up and watched him get into his squad car. "We'll definitely have to do a planned encounter that deals with water. Let's just hope Amy knows how to swim."

"Yeah, let's hope, considering she watches my son."

Nate pulled out of his stall and started toward the road.

She spun her fingers in the air as she put down her binoculars. "Okay. Let's roll."

I couldn't help but laugh as Daisy watched the squad car slowly make its way down main street.

"I'm kind of worried about how much you enjoy this." I pulled out of the parking lot and started back toward town.

"No, slow down. He's coming to a stop sign. We can't let him know we're onto him."

I chuckled. "Or he might be onto us."

"Exactly."

Nate slowly drove down main street and pulled up to a curb to park.

"Oh, no. Oh, no. Oh, no. There's nowhere to go. He's gonna see us drive by."

I loved the thrill and excitement racing through

Daisy's voice. She was really getting a kick out of this, and so was I.

I glanced at Daisy slumping down in the seat. "Well, we live in a small town. I don't think he'll think much of it."

She pounded my shoulder and nodded. "Right there. Park. We'll go grab a coffee and tell Abby what we've learned. It'll make this look like we had this planned all along."

I laughed and found a spot to park as Daisy craned her neck.

"I wonder where Nate's going."

"Hardware store? Café? Antique store? The world is his oyster," I teased.

She frowned and watched Nate wander across the crosswalk. "Another very important point to take note of is whether he's truly single. We can't go hooking up people who aren't, you know, available."

Shaking my head, I chuckled. "That's probably a good rule of thumb."

Daisy gave a quick nod and opened her door, climbing out of the seat. "We have twenty more minutes before Tate wakes up. I promised Amy she could get her nails done when he does, so we have to get home soon."

I shut my door and followed Daisy onto the sidewalk,

sliding my hand over hers as she kept an eye on Nate.

"See? Hardware store."

Daisy slid out her phone and texted someone. "What are you doing?"

She winked at me. "Research."

We wandered into the coffee shop, and I realized singles didn't have a chance at remaining that way in Buttercup Lake, at least as long as the Sunshine Breakfast Club was around.

"Hey, Daisy." Abby waved as we walked up to the counter. "How's it going?"

"Great. If you know what I mean." She waggled her brows. "I'd like a caramel brûlée latte."

Daisy's phone buzzed, and she looked down as I ordered my drink.

"Hmm." Daisy looked over at Abby."

"What's up?"

"Nate bought a few hinges and sample paint, a seafoam green."

Abby nodded as if that told her everything she needed to know.

"What am I missing?" I asked.

Daisy cocked her head and looked at me strangely as we made our way down the counter. "What's making him decide to paint his house? Is he trying to impress someone? Who's coming to see his walls? What does he feel the need to fix all of a sudden?"

My brows quirked. "Well, when you put it that way, it's as clear as mud."

Daisy swept a kiss on my cheek just as the man of the hour walked into the coffee shop.

"Hey, Nate," Abby nearly hollered to warn Daisy.

She spun around to see our sheriff glancing at the bakery section. "I know I said I was only going to do a drink earlier, but I really need that croissant after my swim session."

"Coming up, Nate," Abby said, bending over to pick one out.

A barista called out our drinks as Daisy waved at Nate. "Any fun plans tonight?"

Nate shrugged. "If you call painting a portion of my dining room fun, then yeah?"

"Good times." Daisy nodded. "What made you decide on painting all of a sudden?"

Nate frowned and scratched his chin. "Well, I pulled my chair out too quicky and dented the wall, so I had to replaster and now it's time for paint."

Daisy didn't seem satisfied with that answer, and I realized Nate and Amy had no idea what was coming for them. I squeezed Daisy's shoulders as she took a sip, and she glanced up with a smile before I leaned down to place a quick kiss on the top of her nose.

"I love you, Daisy. So much."

She brushed her nose against mine. "I love you too."

"That. Right there," Nate exclaimed. "That's what I'm looking for."

Daisy grinned. "I'll keep that in mind, Nate."

Chapter Twenty-Nine

Daisy

6 months later

"Who's the good girl?" I scratched my puppy's head right before she rolled over for a belly rub. "You are the cutest little pug I've ever seen."

Tate giggled, sitting in the grass outside as a butterfly landed on the milkweed I'd planted. He pointed at the monarch with rust colors and flapping wings that arched as it fed.

The flower bed was starting to come alive like a brilliant blanket of gems, and Tate loved nothing more than toddling over and popping the flower heads off and crumpling them in his tiny little hands.

"Where's your daddy? He was supposed to be back with a mocha." I gently squeezed Tate's cheek and chuckled. "How can you keep getting cuter and cuter?"

I'd dressed Tate in a tiny pair of khaki shorts and a blue polo. Everything was out of proportion and absolutely adorable.

"Pawtson, leave it." The pug fell into her play pose and grabbed some rose petals. "Leave it, Pawtson."

The pug stared at me with two red rose petals stuck to its lips. "You're more mischievous than a one-year old."

Tate giggled again and somehow fell backward from his sitting position onto his teddy bear. The shock of it all brought tears to Tate's eyes, and I quickly swooped him into my arms.

"It's okay, Tate. You're okay."

Tate's eyes cleared right up and were quickly replaced with a smile as I nuzzled my nose against his.

Amy was getting some shuteye at Brielle and Nick's from her long trip with them last week. They'd spent two weeks in Texas with Tate and flew to Chicago while Amy flew to Buttercup Lake with our little guy.

But tomorrow, Tate turned one, so they'd be flying in

tonight for the festivities.

Our little family was growing, and Pawtson was the best addition. Tate loved staring at her, and he loved that she was on his level. Although Tate had learned to toddle around, he still liked to crawl just as much. Sometimes, when a kid had to get somewhere, it was just faster.

Like now.

Tate rolled onto his knees and started crawling toward Pawtson, who immediately laid down, waiting for her buddy.

"Dada," Tate announced, and my gaze shot to the house where I saw Hunter coming outside with a mocha and a fresh bouquet of flowers.

"Aw, you're too sweet," I called over to Hunter, who beamed as he took us in.

"A new florist shop opened up, and I thought these daisies were perfect for my Daisy."

I stood and wiped the grass off my rear before walking over to Hunter. The vibrant red, orange, and yellow gerbera daisies were perfection, just like this Friday afternoon.

I swept a kiss across Hunter's lips, and he smiled as I whispered, "This day couldn't get any better. I'll go put these in water."

Hunter nodded as his eyes stayed fixed on Tate as he

attempted to stand. Pawtson, who was three months old and seven pounds on her best day, stoically stood so Tate could use her for support if needed.

As I made my way into my kitchen, I glanced back to see Hunter holding Tate in his arms. I'd really come to love and appreciate Nick and Brielle over these last several months, but it certainly couldn't be missed whose son Tate was.

The thought made me chuckle as I filled the vase with water and watched Hunter, Tate, and Pawtson pile into the house. I let the flowers spread into their willowy form and took a sip of my mocha.

"Mmm. Delicious." I glanced at Hunter. "Can you believe Brielle finally realized Buttercup Lake's coffee shop is the best in the world?"

"Buttercup Lake has a way of doing that. We just wear people down."

I chuckled, shaking my head. "So, what's your plan for next week?"

He put Tate down on the rug in the living room and Pawtson happily played with Tate's teddy bear.

"I was thinking of letting Michelle handle the bar."

My brows rose in surprise. "Two weeks in a row?"

He smiled, nodding. "I've been thinking about

opening a place up here too."

"You've mentioned that a few times, but I wasn't sure if you were serious about that."

I followed Hunter into the living room and sat on the couch.

"Oh, no." Hunter groaned. "I forgot his lunch at the house." His eyes connected with mine. "You know, there might be a simple solution to all this back and forth."

My brows quirked. "Oh, yeah? What's that?" I feigned innocence as he laughed, shaking his head.

"Well, let's load up and drive the three houses down."

"I can just stay here." I shook my head.

"No, Purrlock has been very annoying all day. I think she wants to see Pawtson, and I know you won't let her out of your sight."

"Okay. Sounds good. You hear that, Pawtson? We're headed to our vacation home."

Hunter laughed and shook his head, picking up Tate. "I'll go get him fastened in the car seat."

"Okay, I'll be right out."

Hunter shut the door behind him as I grabbed Pawtson's leash and hooked it on her sparkling turquoise collar before I grabbed her favorite dog toy.

We walked out of the house with my mocha in hand,

and I climbed into the front seat of Hunter's car as I looked over at Foxy.

Three weeks ago, she'd taken a turn, and I knew it was over.

But I just couldn't bear to let her go yet, so she stayed in my driveway.

Hunter handed me a blindfold, and I chuckled. "That's a little kinky for the middle of the day, don't you think?"

Hunter burst into laughter and shook his head. "Just put it on."

I stared at the pink blindfold and happily obliged.

Hunter backed out of the driveway, and I started to get a little tense. I wasn't exactly sure what was going on, but it felt like we were headed toward Hunter's house.

As soon as we sped up, we slowed down, and I realized we really were heading to Hunter's. So why the blindfold? My hands started to raise toward it, and Hunter chuckled.

"Keep the blindfold on."

I smiled. "Okay, but I'm pretty sure we're at your house."

Hunter turned off the car and went behind us to unbuckle Tate. Pawtson was getting antsy on my lap as Hunter opened the door. He gave me his hand and helped me out of the car while he held Tate.

"Okay, we're just headed up the walkway a few steps and then I want you to turn around."

"Alright, I can handle that."

I squeezed my little pug and whispered, "Your detective skills are really lacking, Pawtson. You're supposed to be telling me what's going on."

But I did exactly as Hunter said while holding Pawtson tightly. "Aren't blindfolds meant for not knowing where we're going?"

Hunter draped his arm around me while Tate's little foot kicked me in the gut.

"Ooh," I said, laughing, catching his toes so he didn't do it again.

"It's time to remove your blindfold."

I reached up and my fingers clutched the pink fabric. I wasn't sure what to expect.

As I lifted my blindfold off, I stood in shock, staring at a new Subaru in bright red with a huge silver bow on top.

"Uh, Hunter? Why's there a bow on top of a car?" I spun slowly to look at Hunter and Tate as Pawtson wiggled in my arms.

"It's for you, Daisy. I know how sad you were about

Foxy, but you do need a car." He ruffled Tate's hair and brought his gaze to mine. "You drive Tate all around, and it just seemed… practical."

"This isn't practical, Hunter. This is huge. I don't even know what to say." I shook my head. "I can't accept her."

"It's a her?"

I nodded, noticing how the headlights looked like they winked at me. "But it's too much."

"We're a family," Hunter said softly. "What's mine is yours, and what's yours is mine.

"No matter how much you want my naughty gnome, you can't have her," I joked as his words flowed through me. Tate looked tickled to see the big bow on top of the red wagon.

"Go ahead, check it out." Hunter nodded toward the car.

I took a deep breath and made my way toward the car. Part of me felt like I was cheating on Foxy, but when I opened Scarlett's door and the new car smell drifted over me, excitement pulsed through me.

"Hunter, I can't believe this." I set my drink in the amazing drink holder and hopped up on my toes to give him a kiss.

He grinned and opened the back door and put Tate inside as Pawtson hopped over to the passenger seat. Hunter slid in next to his son.

"I have a matching car seat in the garage."

I glanced at Hunter in the rearview mirror and his smile only widened.

"Go ahead, open the console."

"Okay," I said, unsure of what to expect.

As I lifted the lid, I saw a key to his house.

"I know you know the code to get into my house, but I thought this was more official."

I held it tight and smiled as Tate reached his hand out for the key.

"Sorry, buddy. This is a choking hazard." I looked into Hunter's eyes through the mirror and smiled. "I never expected this to happen. I'm just in shock. A car and a key?"

Hunter drew a deep breath and nodded. "Come on, buddy," he told Tate and looked at me. "There's one more surprise."

My emotions were already on overload, so I really couldn't figure out what was next, but I knew today was one I'd never forget.

I followed Tate and Hunter to the front door. He stepped aside and pointed at the lock. "Go ahead, use the key."

Chuckling, I slid the key right into the lock and the door opened.

But I couldn't even believe what I saw in front of me. His foyer had been covered in white flowers. Arrangements covering the walls led me inside, and my pulse quickened.

"What's going on? Is this for Tate's birthday tomorrow?"

Hunter's fingers slid up my spine as he set Tate on the floor and shut the door, and I stared at the flower wonderland.

"This is for you, Daisy." He took my hand as I let Pawtson down onto the floor with Tate, who was already making his way toward the family room.

I spun around, taking in the beauty. "Why would you do this for me?"

He drew a deep breath and smiled. His eyes stayed locked on mine, and I got that familiar flutter of excitement that always drew me to Hunter.

"Today, I wanted to celebrate you. You've been instrumental in Tate's life." He took my hands in his, and my heart skipped a beat. "You deserve all this and more. I love you, Daisy. I always have and always will."

I shook my head as the emotions colliding inside me overwhelmed my senses. I cupped my hands around Hunter and kissed him softly. "You know how to make me feel like the luckiest woman in the world."

"Well, I'm the luckiest man."

Without missing a beat, Hunter got on one knee as I heard a murmur from the kitchen area. I heard a whole bunch of whispering as I watched Tate turn around and follow Purrlock and Pawtson, heading back toward us.

I looked down in Hunter's hand and realized he wasn't holding a ring box. He was holding catnip. I hid my chuckle as the feline and canine led the charge with Tate happily looking like a little drunk fellow as they made their way back toward us.

When Pawtson arrived, I noticed a box tied to her collar. Hunter quickly worked to loosen the bow as Pawtson started rough-housing with Purrlock.

Things were about to get dicey.

Hunter laughed, removing the box and tossing the catnip toy back down the hall as Tate sat down to watch his dad.

Hunter's gaze locked on mine, and he drew a deep breath. "Daisy, since you came into my world, you've made my life incredible. You've brightened every single day of my life. You know how to bring joy into each space you slide into. Tate and I are the luckiest men in the world to have you in our lives." His eyes stayed on mine as he opened the ring box in his hand. "Daisy, will you marry me and complete our family?"

His words swirled around me, washing their meaning into my veins as I stared at Hunter, nodding frantically. I wiped the tears streaming down my face as he stood and slipped the ring onto my finger. Tate pulled on his pants leg and Hunter grinned. "Duty calls."

He swooped Tate into his arms and put him on his hip. Hunter smiled at me, and I knew I had won the lottery. Hunter's lips touched down to mine as his family came down the hallway, cheering. Millie took Tate from his arms as Hunter cupped his palms around my face, kissing me deeper and carving this moment into our family's album of memories I'd always cherish.

When his lips left mine, my pulse still raced, and I turned to look at all the friends and family who'd gathered here to celebrate us, and my heart nearly exploded with love.

"Hunter Knox, you and Tate, Pawtson, and Purrlock are the best things that have ever happened to me. And I can't thank you enough for Scarlett."

His eyes twinkled with mischief. "Who's Scarlett?"

I grinned, resting my head on his chest. "The Subaru sitting outside."

He chuckled, bringing me in for another kiss, and I knew.

I thought back to last Christmas, the Christmas of

Love when my life changed forever and I learned to hope again, to love again.

But I couldn't have opened up my heart if it weren't for the brilliant star in the sky, shining down so brightly and lighting the way for me to find love again.

Dear Readers,

Writing about Daisy and Hunter was so much fun!! There is something about getting to put myself in the town of Buttercup Lake that just makes the words flow. I really hope you had a ball reading this story, and I hope you're looking forward to Nate and Amy's story next in *Smidge of Love*! It will be out in early 2024, so go ahead and add it to your wish list, but there is a pre-order link available too!

I wanted to thank you so much for reading The Sunshine Breakfast Club, leaving reviews, and sharing with your friends and family. It has really given this series life, and it's all because of my fabulous readers. Thank you!

I'm also working away on the Curiosity Bay Series too. Don't miss out on *Heart of Curiosities* and *Wilds of the Heart.*

Warmest wishes,
Karice

KARICE BOLTON BOOKS

CURIOSITY BAY SERIES

HEART OF CURIOSITIES

WILDS OF THE HEART

TEMPTING THE HEART

THE SUNSHINE BREAKFAST CLUB SERIES

DASH OF LOVE

PINCH OF LOVE

SPRINKLE OF LOVE

CHRISTMAS OF LOVE

SMIDGE OF LOVE

CLOUDBERRY INN SERIES

IMAGINING YOU

REMEMBERING YOU

LEAVING YOU

LOVING YOU

MR. MISTAKE SERIES

MR. MISTAKE

MR. ACCIDENT

MR. WRONG

MR. RIGHT

ISLAND COUNTY SERIES
FINDING LOVE IN FORGOTTEN COVE
LOVE REDONE IN HIDDEN HARBOR
TANGLED LOVE ON PELICAN POINT
FOREVER LOVE ON FIREWEED ISLAND
TEMPTING LOVE ON HOLLY LANE
CHANCE AT LOVE ON MYSTIC BAY
IRRESISTIBLE LOVE AT SILVER FALLS
LUCKY IN LOVE ON HOUND ISLAND
MISTLETOE MISCHIEF
ACCIDENTAL LOVE ON MEADOW COVE
LANE
DISCOVERING LOVE ON CRANBERRY LANE
CHRISTMAS ON FIREWEED
IMAGINING LOVE ON WILLOW ROAD
CHRISTMAS CRUSH ON FIREWEED ISLAND
WAITING LOVE AT HAWTHORNE AVENUE
FOREVER CHRISTMAS ON SUGARPLUM
LANE

BEYOND LOVE SERIES
BEYOND CONTROL

BEYOND DOUBT

BEYOND REASON

BEYOND INTENT

BEYOND CHANCE

BEYOND PROMISE

BEYOND the MISTLETOE

SILVER RIDGE SERIES

A HAPPY TRUTH ABOUT LOVE

A LITTLE SECRET ABOUT LOVE

A FUNNY THING ABOUT LOVE

A SURPRISING FACT ABOUT LOVE

A SIMPLE WISH ABOUT LOVE

CHRISTMAS AT SILVER RIDGE

LUKE FLETCHER SERIES

HIDDEN SINS

BURIED SINS

REDEMPTION

MIA

V MAFIA SERIES

BLAKE

DEVIN

JAXSON

THE WITCH AVENUE SERIES

LONELY SOULS

ALTERED SOULS

RELEASED SOULS

SHATTERED SOULS

THE WATCHERS TRILOGY

AWAKENING

LEGIONS

CATACLYSM

TAKEN NOVELLA (A Watchers Prequel)

AFTERWORLD SERIES

RecruitZ

AlibiZ

UprisingZ

BLOOD TORN DUET

BLOOD TORN

BLOOD CURSED

Christmas of Love

KARICE BOLTON BOOKS

CURIOSITY BAY SERIES
HEART OF CURIOSITIES

THE SUNSHINE BREAKFAST CLUB SERIES
DASH OF LOVE
PINCH OF LOVE
SPRINKLE OF LOVE
CHRISTMAS OF LOVE

CLOUDBERRY INN SERIES
IMAGINING YOU
REMEMBERING YOU
LEAVING YOU
LOVING YOU

ISLAND COUNTY SERIES
FINDING LOVE IN FORGOTTEN COVE
LOVE REDONE IN HIDDEN HARBOR
TANGLED LOVE ON PELICAN POINT
FOREVER LOVE ON FIREWEED ISLAND
TEMPTING LOVE ON HOLLY LANE
CHANCE AT LOVE ON MYSTIC BAY
IRRESISTIBLE LOVE AT SILVER FALLS
LUCKY IN LOVE ON HOUND ISLAND
MISTLETOE MISCHIEF
ACCIDENTAL LOVE ON MEADOW COVE LANE
DISCOVERING LOVE ON CRANBERRY LANE
CHRISTMAS ON FIREWEED
IMAGINING LOVE ON WILLOW ROAD
CHRISTMAS CRUSH ON FIREWEED ISLAND
WAITING LOVE AT HAWTHORNE AVENUE
FOREVER CHRISTMAS ON SUGARPLUM LANE

BEYOND LOVE SERIES
BEYOND CONTROL
BEYOND DOUBT
BEYOND REASON
BEYOND INTENT
BEYOND CHANCE
BEYOND PROMISE

Christmas of Love

BEYOND the MISTLETOE

SILVER RIDGE SERIES
A HAPPY TRUTH ABOUT LOVE
A LITTLE SECRET ABOUT LOVE
A FUNNY THING ABOUT LOVE
A SURPRISING FACT ABOUT LOVE
A SIMPLE WISH ABOUT LOVE
CHRISTMAS AT SILVER RIDGE

LUKE FLETCHER SERIES
HIDDEN SINS
BURIED SINS
REDEMPTION
MIA

V MAFIA SERIES
BLAKE
DEVIN
JAXSON

THE WITCH AVENUE SERIES
LONELY SOULS
ALTERED SOULS
RELEASED SOULS
SHATTERED SOULS

THE WATCHERS TRILOGY
AWAKENING
LEGIONS
CATACLYSM
TAKEN NOVELLA (A Watchers Prequel)

AFTERWORLD SERIES
RecruitZ
AlibiZ
UprisingZ
BLOOD TORN DUET
BLOOD TORN
BLOOD CURSED

www.ingramcontent.com/pod-product-compliance
Lightning Source LLC
Chambersburg PA
CBHW021529250626
47154CB00006BA/2030